DILEMMA

Fionn Murphy and
Simon Bramhall

Scalpel Stories

ISBN-978-1-9161915-3-2

Cover design by: Fionn Murphy and Simon Bramhall

Already published in kindle and paperback by
Fionn Murphy and Simon Bramhall

Trick or Treat?
Charity
Just Another Saturday Night

Find out more at www.scalpelstories.com

For
Alexis and Jude

ACKNOWLEDGEMENTS

We both owe so much to so many.
Thank you.
Huge thanks - as always - to our wonderful families
for their unconditional love and support:
Fiona, Jack and George for Simon.
Nick, Lucy, Pippa, James, Alipops, Shirley and Ian for Fionn.

Thank you to all those who have advised, encouraged,
commented and proof read, especially Estelle,
Lynne, Jennie, Chris and James.

CONTENTS

GLOSSARY OF MEDICAL TERMS

A&E:
Accident and Emergency Department, now often termed Emergency Department or ED. A department in a hospital that accepts and treats emergency admissions
Adrenaline:
drug that is given into a vein to increase blood pressure and restart the heart
Anaesthetist:
doctor who puts patients to sleep for operations
Arterial line:
plastic tube that is inserted into an artery (usually the wrist) to closely monitor blood pressure
Ascites:
accumulation of fluid within the abdominal cavity
Autistic:
broad range of conditions characterized by challenges with social skills, repetitive behaviours, speech and nonverbal communication
Autoimmune disease of the liver. Primary biliary cirrhosis:
liver disease caused by the bodies own
antibodies acting against the liver
Bacterial peritonitis (SBP):
primary infection of ascites without an obvious source
Bag of saline:
fluid used intravenously to replace fluid losses in a patient. Saline is salt water
containing sodium and chloride molecules
Biopsy:
removal of a small piece of tissue for examination under a microscope to help with diagnosis

BMI:
body mass index. A calculation that determines whether someone is over or under weight
Cardiologist:
doctor specialising in the heart
Catheterisation:
insertion of plastic tube, in this case into the bladder
Central line:
plastic tube that is inserted into a main (large) vein, often in the neck to provide additional monitoring of vital signs and allow delivery of fluid and drugs
Chemo/chemotherapy:
drug therapy given either by mouth or a drip and is usually used to treat
cancer
Cold ischaemic time:
the period of time following removal from the donor and transplantation into
the recipient when the organ is stored on ice
Coma:
prolonged state of deep unconsciousness
Covid 19:
viral upper respiratory tract infection that can cause severe viral pneumonia and even death in high risk individuals
CPR:
cardiopulmonary resuscitation, using chest compressions and blowing into the lungs to keep someone alive
Crash team:
team of doctors and nurses in a hospital who respond to emergency calls about patients
CT scan:
computer axial tomography is a scan using x-rays that can produce very detailed 3D images of the whole body
DBD (Donation after Brainstem Death):
organ donation when a patient has become brain dead
DCD (Donation after circulatory arrest):

also commonly termed donation after cardiac arrest. Organ donation after withdrawal of life sustaining treatment but not in the presence of brain stem death

Defibrillator:
machine that generates an electric shock to restart the heart

Delayed graft function:
period of time where the transplanted organ does not work at all

Downtime:
period of time that the heart has stopped working before being restarted

Early graft failure:
an organ fails to work at all and function will not recover

Encephalopathy:
a change in the way the brain works which manifests as altered mental state & or
confusion

Extended right hemi hepatectomy with extra hepatic biliary resection and lymph node clearance:
removal of 75% of the liver volume along with the bile duct and surrounding

FY1:
foundation year one doctor. First year of training after medical school

Global cerebral ischaemia:
damage to the brain caused by a period of time when the oxygen supply to the brain was insufficient

Haemorrhoids:
group of veins around the anal canal that can become enlarged and bleed when the
bowels are opened

Hepatologist:
specialist doctor who treats liver disease

High dependency unit (HDU):
area in a hospital with higher levels of nursing and medical care between anICU & a ward

ICU:
intensive care unit. Area in the hospital that provides a higher level of nursing and medical care for the sickest patients
Imaging/Radiology:
department in a hospital that takes x-rays and scans
Immunity:
body's ability to recognise proteins (such as bacteria) as foreign and try and remove them
Immunosuppression:
reduction in the bodies immune system, used in this circumstance to prevent rejection of the transplanted organ
Initial poor function:
a period immediately after transplant when the organ does not work well and additional support is needed
Intubate:
to insert a plastic tube into the windpipe to help with breathing
Irreversible brain damage:
damage to the brain that cannot be repaired
IVC (inferior vena cava):
large blood vessel that returns blood from the lower body to the heart
Kocherisation of duodenum:
dissection to mobilise the duodenum from it's surrounding structures named after the surgeon who first described the technique. Carried out as part of a
Whipple's pancreaticoduodenectomy
Large intestine:
part of the bowel that leads from the small intestine to the anus and is used to turn the waste solid
Liver recipient coordinator (LRC):
experienced specialist nurse who handles the process of liver transplantation
Marginal donor:
organ donor that has additional risk factors that are known to cause poor function or even failure of the organ
Medical Director:

senior doctor who sits on the board of a hospital (or similar) and takes responsibility for all of the doctors who work there

Melanoma:

type of skin cancer

Morphine PCA:

method of controlling pain where a patient is able to use a button on a machine to deliver a defined dose of morphine when they need one

Morphine:

a drug that provides pain relief but is very strong and can be addictive

MRI scan:

magnetic resonance imaging is a scan that uses a large magnet to produce detailed 3D images of the whole body

Oesophageal varices:

enlarged veins at the lower end of the oesophagus (similar to haemorrhoids but at the other end of the gastrointestinal tract) that occur in the presence of

blockage to or reduced blood flow through the liver and can occur in advanced liver disease

Palliative care:

care given to patients in the last stages of their life to ease symptoms and make their passing as comfortable as possible

Patient's Charter:

this set out patients' rights in the NHS and the standards of service they could expect to receive originally published in 1991

Physiotherapist:

profession allied to medicine that provides treatment designed to restore, maintain, and make the most of a patient's mobility, function, and well-being.

Primary dysfunction:

as above but might be prolonged

PTC/percutaneous trans hepatic cholangiogram:

interventional radiology procedure that requires a

large needle to be inserted into the bile ducts via the skin through which radio-opaque contrast is injected to outline the bile ducts and then various treatments can be performed

Public Health England (PHE):

government organisation responsible for: making the public healthier by promoting healthier lifestyles, advising government and protecting the nation from public health hazards

Radiotherapy:

radiation therapy usually applied from a big machine and targeted to a cancer

Registrar (reg):

doctor in training to be a consultant or specialist

Rhythm & output:

terms used to describe how the heart is working

Right renal vein:

blood vessel that returns blood from the kidney to the IVC

Roux loop:

a loop of small bowel that is constructed and used to reconstruct and maintain bowel continuity after various types of surgery

Segments 2 and 3 ducts:

the liver is anatomically divided into 8 segments based on the pattern of blood supply and bile duct drainage. Segments 2 and 3 are in the left lobe of the liver and can be isolated by surgery as a separate entity

Sigmoidoscopy:

telescopic examination of the lower large bowel

Small intestine:

part of the bowel that leads from the stomach to the large intestine and is used for absorption of nutrients

Specialist nurse in organ donation (SNOD):

experienced specialist nurse who handles the process of organ donation

Stage III colon cancer:

cancer of the large bowel that has spread to adjacent lymph nodes but is notyet visible on scans in other areas of the body

STD:
sexually transmitted disease
Steroids:
class of drugs that cause immunosuppression
Stoma bag:
appliance that is used to attach to the skin around where the bowel has been brought out to the skin to catch waste effluent tissue
Trauma Unit:
a hospital that provides services to patients involved in major accidents
Upper GI:
upper gastrointestinal, from the throat to the duodenum but including the liver and pancreas
Ventilate:
to artificially do the breathing for a patient either by hand or by using a machine
Warm machine perfusion:
technique where organs are attached to a machine following removal from a donor and the machine tries to mimic blood flow through the organ to improve preservation. Traditional organ preservation is used by keeping the organs cold but the machine technique keeps them as close to body temperature as possible
Whipple's pancreaticoduodenectomy:
operation to remove the head of the pancreas and surroundings

DILEMMA

CHAPTER ONE

"What's that?"

He leant over, all the better to hear. Behind her the fruit machine began to cough.

"Yer what?"

"I like to know what I'm putting in my body."

The fruit machine began to vomit; metal clattered. A woman screeched.

"Think I'd poison you?"

It was the way she looked at him. The man laughed too loudly and slapped a tea towel against the air which recoiled with pain.

"I'm a landlord, pet. No profit in killing me customers. It's liver and onions, like you ordered."

"I asked for a vegetarian salad."

They both stared at the flat, grey pitted offering on the plate, shivering in thin gravy and snotty onion strings clinging onto the meat to avoid drowning. Those that had been set adrift gazed mournfully back at their compatriots before they sank.

Bloody southerners the man was thinking. Come up here with their posh accents and fancy notions and expect us to fall at their feet. Expect us to be covered in coal dust and treat us like second, no, third class citizens. Why the hell can't they eat normal food like normal people? Just because they all pay a million quid for a house. But, it was not a salad; that much was obvious and she was a (possibly) paying customer.

"Anyone ordered liver and onions?" he brayed aloud without hope. The fruit machine continued to vomit and the people to shout but no one answered.

"Anyone want a liver and onions?" he reluctantly brayed again after a pause just long enough for another couple of onion strings to submerge as the meat began to cool and harden from the outside in. Once pink and plump it had now begun to resemble Anglo Saxon shoe leather.

"I'll have it". The liver momentarily revived, the onions clung on with fresh hope and the gravy trembled - until they saw the body behind the voice. It was Alan.

"Thanks, pet" he wheezed as he eased past the meat-free woman in pursuit of salad and lunged forward to retrieve the trophy from the counter. "Champion. Plenty time before midnight."

As the landlord disappeared to gather for the thin woman with the spritzer, the liver and onions made their way unevenly across the stained carpet towards a small table where sat another woman, thin wristed, alert and fluttery, like a sparrow after a bath. Alan heaved himself down onto the hesitant chair beside her and smiled beatifically. Free grub. Another pint and the new year would arrive in fine style. Hello 2020. Bugger 2019.

The woman at the bar sighed and sipped her tepid sweet spritzer before she edged her own way over to the other side of the room. Her father had barely noticed her absence. He was in his element, surrounded by not-quite friends and acquaintances, many of whom he had only met that evening. He had this knack of meeting people and engaging with them; they loved him, his improbable stories, sharp tongue, filthy language and capacity to absorb vast quantities of alcohol without obvious inebriation. She could tell of course. Years of experience. But he seemed happy, the double whiskies kept coming and with them, his anecdotes, his puns, his racing tips and the way he could name drop without sounding pretentious or condescending. Perhaps it was the trace of the Irish accent that did it, but more likely, it was his charm. He was completely adorable to strangers. A one-legged one-man total entertainment system on wheels. Independent, cheerful, more often than not pissed, he liked to boast about his doctor daughter who wasn't yet too up her own arse to push his wheelchair. Thank God she had only to wear the hair shirt for a few days; the warden managed him beautifully the rest of the year but took time off over the Christmas season. Insisted on it. So, she and her half-sister took it in turns to stand in. Maybe one year they might even do it together her father had once suggested slyly, poised on the edge of sobriety.

"I doubt it" she now decided to herself and wondered what Fergus was doing. Was he busy? You could never predict what would happen on-call in a big hospital, especially on New Year's Eve. What did he do with himself when she was 'oop north as he called it, being the dutiful daughter?

Fergus Crombie was very much on-call, in every sense. The girl was only a student nurse but none the worse for that: obliging, a little overawed, very compliant and on site. Women like her were so accommodating. Order in something other than pizza, a little old-fashioned courtesy – holding doors open, always insisting 'after you', requesting permission to kiss her and the rest just fell into place. It was a little too easy for his taste but he was on duty, and who knew when he might be summoned? No time to waste and only a single bed in the overnight hospital on-call accommodation so one had to have someone slender. He would not give the woman with the warm spritzer a thought until she texted him at midnight to wish him a happy New Year. Then he would become extremely busy but would manage to squeeze a moment out of the ongoing mayhem to call her back, briefly, just enough time to suggest he loved her but that he had to go. Such a shame about her name. Who in their right mind called someone Betsy? How could anyone look at a new-born baby and decide that it should be a Betsy? Servants, big-breasted, apple-cheeked milk maids with cankles, lugubrious over weight Labradors or Enid Blyton schoolgirl heroines were called Betsy, not anaesthetists with aspirations to consultancy and medical directorship.

Betsy's salad arrived, in a state of despair. It stared mournfully up at her from the plate on which it lay flat and limp alongside the cutlery swaddled in a paper napkin.

"Come on" it seemed to say; "let's get this over with".

She pushed it aside, untouched, with its escort of mayonnaise sachets, to wither and die. She'd have another drink instead. More calories of course, but more uplifting and if she hadn't eaten anything on the last day of the old year, which would be the case if she eschewed the salad, then she could have a treat to kick off the new one. Maybe even something sweet. Heartened by hunger pangs and the prospect of forbidden carbohydrate she was fortified and leant back in her chair while her father held court. As he performed, she took the opportunity to scrutinise her surroundings. Ever the anaesthetist: watching, monitoring, judging; silent and ultimately, in charge. Even lead surgeons had to obey anaesthetists.

The man with the liver and onions was opposite, some way across the room, seated at a larger wooden table than theirs although his bulk made the table seem small and the woman seated next to him, even smaller. Tiny. Birdlike she was twittering at him and although the words were inaudible the message was clear. She was cross; he was eating too much. Hadn't he already had enough? What, with the ale and the crisps – she was jabbing a bony figure at the empty packets but he took no notice. Only when he had cleared the plate, wiped his chin on the still folded paper napkin and emptied his pint glass did he acknowledge her and then it was to burp. His whole body shuddered with the effort and although she could not actually hear it, Betsy witnessed the birth of the belch in the pit of the belly then watched its progress into being - up, up the tight chest into the stretching neck, along the throat and then out, a triumphant explosion through the gravy stained mouth into the world, rejoicing loudly in its new found freedom.

"Pardon".

"Alan Beale. You should be ashamed" chirruped the bird.

"Only air, pet. Better out than in. Want another?" he said, indicating her full glass, knowing that she would refuse.

The television had taken over from the now exhausted fruit machine, emptied of its contents which watched bemused as all the cash it had so recently regurgitated found its way across the bar counter into the till as the victor celebrated. Mein host tried not to gloat but pressed home his advantage.

"Nearly midnight, folks. Time to top up."

Alan heaved himself out of his chair, empty glass in hand and contemplated the journey to the now crowded bar. He'd have to wait when he got there; the staff were hard at it ahead of Big Ben's midnight chimes on the telly but he did not like to be rushed, not even for a pint. Anyway, the chimes would always be there; one new year was much the same as an another at his time of life. But hell, it was hot in there. Perhaps he'd go outside first for a sneaky fag. Norma, the name of the little bird, wanted him to give up; went on and on like a bloody dripping tap about it until he had vaguely promised to cut down, but not said when. Besides, what difference would it make? He'd smoked since he was a lad; they all did, him and his mates. You couldn't survive in them shipyards without a smoke.

"You alright, pet? You look a bit peaky."

God, she was fussing again. Meant well, she did, but never stopped.

"Stop maitherin' pet. It's warm in here. I'll step out for a bit air and be champion."

It really was hot and he felt sweat on his face. That bloody indigestion was back again, he could feel the familiar band of burning in his belly rising and lacing his chest, like someone tugging the strings of a fiery corset to make him look thinner. No wonder he was short of breath. He began to gasp, softly at first and then loudly, desperately, as the tightening band clutching his body squeezed and crushed so that all the air disappeared and he found he was swallowing his own throat which was difficult because the nausea in his stomach was thick in his windpipe and all he wanted to do was vomit his way back to breath and fresh air and light.

"Alan!"

Big Ben detonated the first of the twelve; eyes and ears focused on the bellow as it resounded from the TV screen, ringing out into the pub, reverberating across the world. Alan fell to the stained carpet floor and never heard the second. The little bird squawked and twittered, fluttered her wings and flew down beside him. No one else had noticed.

CHAPTER TWO

The excitement, the build-up, the climbing crescendo as the countdown lifted off and the numbers fell, like skittles, tumbling away with the old to embrace the new. Glasses rose, spirits soared, strangers embraced, mein host beamed and offered his staff a free drink, but just one, mind. Betsy's father spearheaded celebrations from his portable throne, waggling his knee-stump in the air and stamping his only foot on the floor, an invitation to the dance as a conga formed around him. Betsy declined a hot handed sweaty-palmed invitation to participate and stayed in her seat, slightly aloof, smiling tightly and wondering how long it would be before they could leave. No time soon looking at the state of Dad; he had the craic upon him. It would be a long night. She looked at her phone. Nothing from Fergus but that was not a surprise although she felt disappointed, then guilty. Neediness really annoyed him. She began to text. The conga picked up pace and people: bowed bodies swaying, knees bent, legs angled akimbo, disjointed, ungainly, like an overfed snake with a bad attack of palsy. Longer and longer, louder and louder, fuelled by drink and hysteria. Only when it got to the other side of the room and Alan, embedded in a broken chair and a broken wife, did it stop. Suddenly, like a motorway pile up, body upon body, momentum suspended but unable to stop.

"Bloody hell, man. What's happened?"

Norma didn't know - he just fell over. All of a sudden; no warning. Just went down and hadn't moved since.

Gone down he certainly had and it had been a bumpy ride. The big man had fallen forward onto the table as his knees had softened to nothing and his legs had folded. The table had stood firm, fixed on four sturdy legs, determined not to fail in its duty but it had not been easy and it had been severely shaken, bounced, almost upended. The chair had not been so fortunate and now lay in severed disarray, its legs broken from its seat and its carcase prone on the floor, much as Alan himself lay. He had come to rest on his back having fallen onto the table face first with such impact that he had been twisted around so that although on his back, his legs were tucked beneath him. His face was bloody and swelling as they watched; blood seeped from his nostrils and misaligned nose. The hand in which he had held his glass was clutched into a fist, as an aged baby and it looked as if he had wet himself. But that might have been the contents of the little bird's overturned glass, now nestling on the carpet after flinging its amber liquid up into the air, over the table and onto the body below. It continued to drip, crying silently within the noise and movement all about it.

"Ted!"

Betsy's father did not hear. The conga dismembered and splintered and the voice shouted, much louder.

"Ted! Your lass's a doctor?"

"Aye."

"Get her over here."

Even as she approached Betsy could tell it was serious. It was something about the way the man lay and an instinct born of years in hospital theatres. Anaesthetists developed not so much another sense but an indefinable moment of dark hollowness in the pit of the stomach when there was trouble. The motionless patient in their care could neither speak nor communicate but the Sandmen – the good ones – knew, just knew, when things were going wrong.

"Call an ambulance" she shouted at no one and everyone. "Move!"

The dismantled conga in a circle around the broken man widened and split to let her through. The little bird fluttered to one side and stood up. Someone stood next to her and put their arm around her shoulders. Afterwards it seemed to Norma that it all had all happened in slow motion, from the moment Alan had stood up and belched to the point where he was taken away from her on a small-wheeled collapsible stretcher barely able to support his weight. She had thought it would not be able to move – the paramedics had had to push really hard to get the wheels to roll over the carpet and started to sweat with the effort .... Alan had been sweating. Oh, why had she not realised? Done something?

"Is he your husband?" Betsy addressed the frightened bird who nodded. "What's his name?" she asked, gently, and strained to hear the feather soft reply.

Then on her knees, as if in supplication, Betsy bent over him.

"Alan? My name's Betsy. I'm a doctor" she said as she felt his thread pulse and checked his irregular respiration as he gasped for air. She examined his battered face and gory twisted nose, noticed the hard-curled fist and the empty glass which had fallen with him then rolled some distance away bearing testament, as if it was needed, to the velocity of his fall.

"Please tell me what happened" Betsy order-asked the little bird someone introduced as Norma; Norma Beale. And so, Norma, for the second time of many more that night, described how Alan had just stood up then fallen down, all at once, heavy like and never said one word of complaint about anything except that he felt a bit warm.

"Help me turn him over."

He was alive but completely out of it. Betsy had undone his collar and the top button of his shirt, clean on for the occasion, still displaying loving creases made by Norma's iron but stretched to breaking point over the man's belly over which the buttons were panting and straining, desperate for release. There was no tie to undo – Alan was not a man who wore ties, except for funerals. His jacket had been taken off hours ago and hung sadly over the back of a chair on the other side of the table, watching events with limp helplessness. Could not even get the folded square of an old-fashioned cotton handkerchief out of a pocket to wipe the man's nose.

Betsy and unknown hands shifted the body onto its side into the recovery position. The surrounding furniture was hastily shoved out of the way creating a macabre stage: audience participation drama. Improvisational theatre ringed by revellers in various states of inebriation but no laughter. Beyond them the television continued to blast out the noise of celebration, exploding fireworks, party poppers and corks, bagpipes, party joy, *bon homie*, joy, optimism and goodwill to all men.

"The ambulance's on its way. Turn that bloody thing off!"

Someone behind the bar cut the television and even the fruit machine seemed subdued, ashamed, more flashing lights and pulse than an invitation to play. Nothing to play for anyway, not since it had been emptied. The sudden quietness fell like snow, muffling the air, coating the world with soft plumage; cold. Only the muted voice Norma telling Betsy about her husband's medical history and habits broke the stifled atmosphere.

From afar the eagle screech of a siren froze the softness into shards, louder and louder, hope and menace in every encroaching shriek. Norma and Betsy alone did not turn to look as the double doors to the pub flung open and two green-clad bodies hurled themselves through, one listing a little to the side on account of the baggage she was carrying. Her partner led the way; the waves parted and he was on his knees beside Alan in a second. Norma was shaking; trembling. The arms around her tightened. Betsy brought the paramedics up to speed about the patient, neatly summarising his condition and medical history: hypertension controlled by medication, border-line diabetic and a long-term smoker. Only then did she clarify that she was in fact a doctor and so yes, she did know what she was talking about.

"I'd say it's a heart attack" she finished.

They agreed. It looked very much like it. They would take over now? Of course, and she edged back to let the paramedics get on with it.

"Blood pressure low. Oxygen, ventilate, then intubate."

Had he complained of any discomfort, pain, that sort of thing? Norma shook her head as the man in green spoke, then considered for a moment before whispering so quietly he could barely hear her,

"Only indigestion after too much Christmas dinner but nothin' a Rennies couldn't mend. Nothin' else. A bit wind now 'n then... He'd promised to give up the smokes ..."

"He's arrested!"

"Commencing CPR" said the female paramedic even as she started hand-on-fist thumping Alan's hefty chest. She lifted herself up after the first pummelling and counted the seconds as her colleague ripped open the man's shirt. The buttons sighed with relief. "Oxygen!" she panted, as if in need of it herself as she resumed her rhythmic pushing and releasing; stop; push; release; stop; push; release.

"He's not responding. Got to shock him. Adrenaline. 1 mg now and repeat as required."

Cue the man in green who was attending to the baggage which had been deposited alongside the scene of the drama like an untidy prop. While the woman kept up the CPR and the audience accompanied her every move, the defibrillator was pulled out and began to charge up. As its high-pitched whine soared into life, the male paramedic unceremoniously jabbed adrenaline into Alan's lifeless arm.

"Stand back. All clear."

It sounded like an industrial sized staple gun going off except that instead of fixing Alan to the ground it made him jerk away from it before falling heavily back, horribly lethargic and unresponsive. Norma gasped. Everyone else gasped and stood, open mouthed, almost as shocked as the body in front of them.

One. ... Two .... Three...

"And again. Stand clear."

Another staple-gun shot. Another gap. All eyes now followed those of the woman with the mechanical heart beat in her hands as she watched the screen dumped on the floor beside her, incongruous on the jaunty beer-stained carpet; a lurid backdrop to life or death.

She leant back from the body and raised her hands in triumph.

"Rhythm and output restored" she said, as much for the edification of the audience as her own relief. "Welcome back, Alan."

Norma gasped again and fluttered inside the arms that held her together. No, she could not crouch down and cuddle her husband; they had to get him to hospital as soon as they could.

"But he's never been ill in his life!" She was protesting. Where were they taking him? Why was this happening? What was the matter with him?

"It looks as if he's had a heart attack, pet" the man in green said. "But they'll know for sure when he gets to hospital. He'll be in good hands" he added, as if this was some sort of consolation. Then, completely disregarding Norma, he and his partner set about preparing Alan for transportation.

"Blues and twos for you, bonny lad" the man said to his cargo as Norma's dearly beloved was squeaky-wheeled out of the pub.

"Which hospital?" Betsy called after them.

"The RI" he shouted back, bent over with the exertion of pushing the heavy burden as he was halfway through the door. The words reverberated around the pub in his wake as he disappeared and the doors shut behind him.

CHAPTER THREE

"Will he make it?"

"I don't know, Dad. It's impossible to tell. But they'll do everything they can for him. He's lucky that the hospital's so close and he's in good hands."

"Poor bugger" was Ted's lament and those around him nodded in agreement. So much for a Happy New Year. With Alan's departure went every vestige of enjoyment and pleasure; drinks were left either unfinished or hurriedly downed with a sense of desperation, as if the process of clearing the once celebratory alcohol might somehow revive earlier optimism and hopes. It did not. Nor did it dispel the sound of Norma's weeping which lingered long after she had left the premises to be driven in pursuit of the ambulance to the hospital. No one wanted her to go with Alan, least of all the paramedics. They did not know what might happen on the way. Betsy had tried to explain this to Norma who, quite simply, did not understand. Her Alan had never been ill before; he wouldn't know what was happening without her there to explain. They had never been separated, not in all the time they'd been married and it would be their Ruby wedding anniversary this year. Forty years married and they'd known each as bairns: grown up together.

The owner of the arms that had folded around Norma was the one who put her in a car and drove as fast as he could to the

Royal Infirmary in the centre of the city. He would have liked to follow the ambulance but blue lights had privilege and *carte blanche* over red lights and bus lanes. And the roads were busy – why man, it was ridiculous! At this time of night! Not with vehicles though, but semi-clad, fully-cut New Year's Eve revellers spilling out of one set of pubs and clubs en route to the second, or underground to the Metro for last trains that they had missed. Thrown out of that underworld they had risen up to the earth's surface to crowd once more over the streets, pavements and alleys that radiated out from the Monument. The whole of the city centre had become intoxicated; sense was numb, vision had doubled and touch was concentrated mostly on bottles and/or someone one else's flesh. Preferably both. Sound, however, was alive and well and very much in the ascendant.

"How can they not hear us?" the paramedic driving the shrieking flashing ambulance shouted through to her colleague in the back. "Or see us?"

She was swerving much more than she would have liked but there were bodies all over the place; pavements and streets were as one, a single thoroughfare for feet and fun. In the back of the vehicle her colleague was struggling. Alan was strapped onto the stretcher but even that was trembling with the violent motion. Its occupant however, noticed nothing, his torso simply following the shivers and shakes of his bed as if they were one, somehow joined together below the NHS blanket covering his legs and belly. The tubes extending from his uncovered arms swung gaily to and fro, streamers on a boat on a swelling sea, reaching further and further across the deck as if to touch hands with the other side.

"Can't we go any faster?" replied the other paramedic, braced against the sway but still finding himself falling in and out of Alan's inert body. "His blood pressure's droppin'."

"What?" howled the driver, narrowly missing two girls in the middle of the one-way street just outside the university. One of them was apparently meditating lying down while her friend stood over her attempting what seemed to be the art of levitation. Neither was wearing much in the way of clothes and three shoes were to be seen ornamenting the pavement. The fourth was in the gutter with a handbag with which it seemed to be arguing.

"His BP's droppin'. Get a move on."

This the driver did hear and she accelerated with such vigour that even the stretcher seemed in danger of making a run for it.

"Radio ahead and get the crash team on standby" the man in the back shouted as he lunged backwards.

"I'm on it" she returned as the man plunged forward again. "Bloody New Year revellers. They're all over the place".

"They'll be in A&E next" the man informed Alan over whom he was now leaning. "It's always the same, every single year."

The ambulance finally turned into the long drive up to the emergency department entrance and, accelerator down, siren singing, lights staining the air iridescent fractured blue, it made a final dash for the finish line. By the time the brakes had screamed themselves hoarse as the wheels came to a stop, steaming and panting with effort, the doors had opened both of the ambulance and the hospital building. Alan's weighty trolley was easy to unload with the merciful assistance of gravity and although it was slow to gather momentum when the paramedics began to push, once the small wheels had got the hang of the extra burden upon their axles they rose to the challenge with aplomb. No time even to squeak; they soon had their cargo safely inside the automatic double doors in a time that impressed even themselves.

But no time to crow. They went straight into the arms of the hovering crash team and then, escorted by many hands, into the acute treatment area where Alan would be transferred onto something else with wheels but more fixed; stable, attached to a forest of pipes, wires, tubes, monitors which were connected to things with yet more pipes, wires, tubes and even bigger monitors.

"BPs right down. Critical. Looks like he might arrest. Again. He's called Alan Beale. The wife's on her way." The two paramedics spoke as a double act even while propelling the trolley across the floor. It was impossible to distinguish who said what especially amidst the sound of slapping Crocs and the rustle-swish of plastic aprons which accompanied the tune of the wheels and the song of the crash team.

"Bring him through. Ventilate. Intubate. Adrenaline. Bloods."

"He's arresting!"

Then one voice, not louder but more in control - that of the on-call registrar – the reg - used to leading the team and giving instructions, knowing that by the time he spoke they were probably already being implemented:

"Stand by for CPR. Page the on-call cardiologist – Dr Fraser. Now."

More hand over fist thumping on Alan's battered chest which was now starting to bruise and dent. More counting, some muttered, some silent; all measured but increasingly less hopeful. The backdrop of the monitor, flat-lining. A single green line flowing across its face, emitting a high-pitched unbroken whine like an endless sigh; the last hurrah.

"Hell. ... I think we may have lost him but we'll have one more go."

So once again, another defibrillator, another place, another stand by to shock and the staple gun shot its bolt.

Once.

Twice.

And then the monitor changed its tone, struck a different chord as the green line started to bounce and jump across the screen.

"Yes!"

"Sorry! I came as fast as I could." Dr Fraser prided himself on his fitness and enviable BMI but even he, a man who jogged when it was fine and rode an exercise bike in the back bedroom in front of the TV when it was not, had found the sprint along unforgiving hospital floors at the back end of his shift a step too far. Damn his shoes. It had been his wife's idea.

"It's New Year's Eve – smarten yourself up a bit" she had said. "Wear those new shoes you got in the sales last year. You haven't worn them yet." I do my best she thought in sorrow.

Never again he rued. Never again would he renounce the glory of well-worn trainers, even if they were a bit blood stained; you never knew when you would have to leg it down a hospital corridor.

"He's back with us." A small note of victory in the voice of the reg by way of greeting for the breathless cardiologist, but nothing to boast about; everyone there knew what had happened and what the consequences might yet be.

"Nice work" William Trafalgar Fraser (known always and only as Bill except to his wife) exhaled.

"Family?"

"Wife's in reception."

"His second arrest tonight?"

The reg nodded. They all knew what this meant but no-one liked to accept it, never mind put voice to it. Bill Fraser knew what those faces around the patient were saying but there was still work to be done. His voice was steady; he was a practical man despite the best efforts of his wife to make him into an intellectual and an eminent local social fixture. He loved his job almost as much as his foul-tempered diabetic cat and enjoyed being at the hospital a great deal more than at home. The only person who seemed not to know this was his wife of twenty-one years – neither of them knew how.

"We need to stabilise him." Bill used the first-person plural whenever he could; they were all in it together. Everything was team work in the NHS, in spite of the managers. "Then run bloods and scan him. I'm concerned..." he spoke for them all, "that the repeated downtime may have caused brain damage."

There. It had been said. Now, move on.

"If that's the case and it's a global cerebral ischemia as I fear then there are some hard decisions to make. What's his wife called?"

A brief consultation with the notes at the end of the bed produced the answer and then a pause after which the reg wanted to groan.

"Married forty years" he sighed, as if delivering a still birth.

"Oh God. Let's get the test and scan results before we talk to her."

After the events in the pub it had been much easier than Betsy feared to get her father home. He was subdued but it was difficult to know whether that was as a result of Alan's collapse or the whisky. It was a relief to push the wheelchair up the ramp to the front door and Ted was at least sober enough to press the right button on the key fob to activate the automatic release. As the door eased servilely inward, endlessly deferential, ever obliging, no tip required, Ted addressed his daughter. When his time came to be planted, he said, he didn't want any fuss.

"Save the money and have a party instead."

Betsy steered him into the living room. It was the same conversation they always had at this time of year. Outside the sound of fireworks had all but ceased and the room felt small and oppressive, as if they were insulated from the outer world and they were the only people able to move or make sound. It was that time of night when the world seemed to stop and slumber, hibernation while reality recovered its energy for the day to come. There was always a moment in the hospital like this, sometimes so brief it passed unnoticed but occasionally much longer, when lights dimmed, movement ceased, doors stayed closed, corridors were empty, noise was hushed and even the walls seemed to be asleep. Betsy wondered what Fergus was doing while she replied, the same as ever, that her father was talking nonsense, had years yet, would outlive them all just to have the party himself but yes, if that was what he wanted of course that's what they'd do.

"You're not listening to me."

She denied it so vehemently that he knew she was lying.

"What's his name then?"

Betsy told him.

"Fergus. Crombie? Like the coat?"

"Like the coat and yes, he's an anaesthetist, like me." She rushed on to prevent her father from finding fault; why, oh why did she always seek his approval? "He's an ex-marine; practised medicine on the frontline in war zones all over the world and now divides his time between the hospital and the helicopter and ambulance services. He only spends some of his time in the hospital... I think he needs more variety and excitement." She omitted to mention his appetites, including the fast cars funded by his very lucrative private practice attending to the cosmetic needs of much of the Midlands.

There was a silence. Betsy was admiring the pace and adventure of Fergus's life compared to her own, not that the hospital wasn't interesting of course and you never quite knew what might happen next, but it wasn't often thrilling and never sexy. More pressure than passion; not so much airborne and blue lit but down to earth, grounded, often grubby and always exhausting. Fergus was like the cavalry – swept in, swept up, swept out and left someone else to clear up afterwards. Even his stints in theatre were somehow less routine and more exciting than everyone else's. He was a voyage, a journey and she wanted to travel with him. Ted on the other hand, was wondering when his lass was going to tell him something sensible about the man in her life, like his age and his marital status. She was a canny lass, no question, but a fool.

The silence continued. Eventually Ted asked what time she was heading off back to the smoke. Did she really have to go? Yes, she did. She was on duty the following day so she wouldn't leave it too late; the traffic on bank holidays was always so dreadful and she'd have to get a good night's sleep before she went into work. Shame she was on an early but it couldn't be avoided. (She wasn't and it could). But she'd be in touch with him and if there were any problems all he had to do was let her know and she'd be there in no time.

She'd make sure she ate properly, wouldn't she? You needed stamina and muscle for a job like hers and she was looking a bit thin Ted said. Too thin. He worried about her. Thus, began yet another New Year.

CHAPTER FOUR

"I'll do it."

The registrar spoke quietly, resigned weariness in every syllable. Despite their low volume they stood out against the raucous backdrop; in A&E the waiting room was a riot. Literally. Just as the paramedics had predicted, the next incumbents were indeed those happy revellers who had been hugging the pavements and roads, clinging onto bottles, cans, flesh, lamp posts and their determination to celebrate. Now they had found their bruised, sometimes blood soaked and always inebriated way to the RI emergency department where the party continued unabated, fuelled by the occasion and the close proximity to functioning toilets – complete with toilet paper - for which the disorderly queue was rapidly descending into the belligerence of those about to burst.

Bill Fraser pitied the reg who was relatively new in post which was why he had drawn the short straw and got New Year's Eve. Next year he would be wiser.

"I'll talk to her." Bill said. "It sounds like you've got enough to do out there."

He was speaking of Norma and already planning on finding a private corner somewhere to tell her about Alan, away from the escalating noise and tension in the adjacent waiting area. Soon the irritation would break out, like eczema, be rubbed and agitated and scratched until the skin broke and the fighting started. Then the blood flowed. Always the same, every year: alcohol fuelled aggression which ended with a police punch up and the medical staff hiding from their own patients. People were at least still singing though, which meant he had time to remove the poor almost-widow away from that mayhem. That he was removing her into another form of chaos was not lost on him. It was all part of the job but if he was honest, he would rather have been dealing with the waiting room which was so alive.

They were sitting together, three of them. The young nurse was there for 'support', although what support such a young lass could give her was lost on Norma. Why, the girl was no older than a bairn. It was a bit of a squeeze in the small cheaply furnished room which was ludicrously over lit from above by a neglected strip light. More grey than white, except where a blackened crack had split one side revealing a wire thin line of sharp light; all along its length lay the corpses of long deceased insects, visible in murky shape only through the brittle plastic funeral pyre upon which they had come to rest. The brightness of the room was so inappropriate thought Bill. News like his should be delivered in subdued, soft lighting that soothed not screeched and bawled.

"I'm so sorry Mrs Beale – Norma. The test and scan results confirm the very thing we were afraid might happen. Your husband has suffered irreversible brain damage."

Norma had not noticed the harsh light, or the furnishings or indeed, even that she was in a different room. She saw only the thin man sitting before her, leaning forward in her direction as if to put out his hands and catch a thrown ball that might arrive at any second. He was a nice man, she had decided that when she first met him and he introduced himself as Bill Fraser, a heart doctor, not some fancy title that she would not understand. And she liked the name Bill; it was an ordinary, no airs and graces sort of a name. Her grandfather had been called Bill and he had been such a lovely man, a proper bonny lad.

"But he might get better? People come out of comas, even after years, don't they? I've read about it." She stopped. Pleaded with her eyes. Bill so wanted to look away but kept his gaze fixed on hers. She continued, as if talking might make a difference; if she could convince the doctor then everything would be alright. "He's strong, my Alan. Never been ill in his life. If anyone can come through this he can."

"It's not a question of strength, Norma. Your husband isn't in a coma." He saw that she was listening, but would she understand? "Unfortunately, his condition is much more serious than that. When his heart stopped, twice, the brain became starved of blood and was damaged beyond repair. He's only being kept alive by the machinery supporting him and enabling him to breathe."

"Twice?"

"The first time was in the pub when you were there and then it happened again when he arrived here, in the hospital... Do you remember me telling you that? ... In the Emergency department ... when you arrived?"

"Yes."

No, she didn't. It was obvious.

But now she did seem to have heard. The tone of her voice changed. It had become less accommodating and assenting; doubt and fear coloured her words.

"What are you sayin' doctor?"

"That there's nothing else we can do for him. Further treatment is futile."

"Futile?"

"Nothing will be achieved by further treatment."

"But how do you know? It's too soon to say something like that. Why, he only got ill last night and he's never been ill in his life so how can this happen? It's not right, not my Alan. You must have made a mistake."

She put her hand to her mouth in shock – had she really said that? To a doctor? In her world people didn't challenge the word of doctors, or nurses, or lawyers or professionals or the police or even a traffic warden but this was Alan, her Alan, and she had to fight. What was this man saying? That they would have to turn the machines off?

Yes. Apparently, that was exactly what he was saying.

It was a terrible shock and she would need time to process it; he was so very sorry. They were there to help in any way they could ... But what use was that when they couldn't bring Alan back? Except that he hadn't gone, not really; he was still there, in that bed with all those machines and tubes, lying on his back propped up on pillows just like he did at home in the morning, snuffling in half-sleep while she made them both a cup of tea. Only at home he wore pyjamas and here his chest was there for anyone to see, covered with round corn plaster things with wires attached. It would hurt when they pulled the plasters off, especially where it was hairy and he would hate that. He could be such a babby about small hurts; cuts, grazes, that sort of thing. Oh, that time when he had picked up the pot of stew on the table and burned himself. It was straight out of the oven – she had told him when she put it down, 'don't touch the pot it's hot' but did he listen? Tiny little burns they were, hardly anything but you'd have thought he had been caught by one of those welding torches they used in the Yard the way he'd gone on. Yet he'd never complained about the Yards and the danger and never even missed a day's work, not even when he'd had the flu. Why was that?

"Norma?"

She found she was crying. When had that started? The little nurse gave her a tissue, then the whole box. When all she wanted was one of Alan's hankies, blue-rinsed white, folded and ironed, straight out of his left trouser pocket where they lived, always unused. She had washed, ironed and folded him a clean hanky every day of their married life, just in case. And now here was an 'in case' and she couldn't have it.

"Are you sure there is no-one to be with you? A relative or a friend?"

"No. We never had bairns. It's just Alan and me."

Silence.

Norma had heard herself speaking as if she was far away and the voice was not hers but another Norma, the one-before, as if she was watching someone who looked like her and even sounded like her, but who was different. Somewhere else. She felt as if she was floating, about to collide with the ceiling and she would have to put out her hands to push herself away from the strip light, like tapping at a balloon in the air then watching it saunter dreamily off in another direction. Below her sat the doctor and the nurse and a lady she knew was her, but wasn't. That Norma had gone.

She could not decide if she wanted someone to tug the balloon string and pull her down. She ought to be anchored, but it was so much easier up here.

The doctor was talking to the lady. Couldn't he see she had gone? He was saying something about their excellent support network and how he would get someone to be with her as soon as he could. They had people – marvellous people – available twenty-four/seven (whatever that meant) who would understand and help her in all sorts of ways. They were trained and informed and could guide her through the practicalities of the situation as well as helping her to deal with her emotions. Really? And the little nurse continued to sit and gaze – so kindly - at the lady's face which was wet and her nose was all snotty. So she pulled out another tissue and handed it to the woman who was crying while the doctor was on his phone, one of those mobiles that showed you the person you were talking to so that you could have a conversation with them, just like they were standing in front of you. Except he wasn't talking he was sending a message and she heard a ping when it was sent. The sound flew up into the air like an insect and buzzed around the strip light with her.

Now the lady was holding the tissue but not using it. She was snivelling, the leakage from her eyes mixing with the drizzle from her nose onto the front of her blouse which was getting all wet. Her best blouse, the one she had worn to see in the New Year. She must have been there some time for it to have become that wet but it was impossible to know how long. Where had Time gone? She heard the woman speak and stopped moving so that she could clearly make out the words coming from her mouth.

"He's not in any pain, is he?"

Oh, she did hope not. She would not want her Alan to be in pain.

"No. He can't feel anything at all. His brain has stopped working completely so his body has stopped as well."

That was a relief. But what did the doctor mean, his body had stopped?

At that moment the door opened and another person floated in, softly, in spite of her size. She seemed to fill the already crowded room and Norma was aware of herself being squeezed up against the ceiling, alongside the strip light which was strangely comforting, like lying beside Alan in bed.

"This is Grace" the doctor said to the lady with the tissue as the big woman plump-thumped herself into a seat. Norma felt the pressure on the chair and heard it groan but she was the only one; everyone was looking at the other Norma, the one with the wet blouse. She looked so sad. Norma's heart ached for her. Grace did not speak; not one word. Instead she reached over and took both of the sad lady's hands into her own and held them.

Then Norma felt herself drifting away from the strip light, which seemed sorry to see her go. Another time perhaps? she felt it say but answering was impossible because she was already far below it, watching it recede. And she felt as if she was empty and needed to breathe but could not because the air was rushing past her and would not stop, not even for her to catch some in her lungs.

"There now, pet. You let it out."

And her lungs were full and she was howling. Yelping into the sharp scratchy brightness but Grace was still holding her hands and would not let go – would not let her float away and be safe but was making her sit on the chair, park her feet on the stained floor, wear the wet blouse. Now she was cold and her face was covered in slimy tears which would not stop and oh, how it hurt. It hurt so much that all she could do was bawl like a babby – broken, body shaking, sobbing.

CHAPTER FIVE

The cold light of New Year's Day. The infant year resting now after the trauma of its birth, all pain forgotten as it was cradled in hope and swaddled in good intentions. The irony was not lost on Bill Fraser.

"She's agreed that the support has to be turned off" he said to the reg as the night shift was coming to a close and they were preparing to handover. They were sitting in the staff room, nursing cups of metallic vending machine coffee, only slightly infected by the smell of urine and alcohol which filled the corridors and waiting room. The cleaners and, to some extent the porters, had begun the clear up operation with as much heroism and determination as any surgeon, though with less recognition and a great deal less remuneration.

"Grace?" the reg's eyebrows asked.

"I don't know how she does it" Bill said. He and the little nurse had crept, unnoticed, out of the over-lit room leaving Norma with the enigmatic Grace. There was something about her, impossible to define but in her presence, people released emotions unknown even to themselves. Grace seemed to absorb their pain, to suck it into her own soft body so that they gave more and more until they were exhausted, spent, able to breathe normally and then, eventually, to pick up the torn pieces of a changed life. Then Grace would speak; they would hear and what was more, they would listen.

"What about ... organ donation?" the reg asked, tentatively. Timing was everything.

Bill shook his head.

"Not yet. It's too soon but it'll have to be discussed. We've got to let her come to terms with her husband's death before we start on that one. I'll get in touch with the organ donation nurses though, so that they're prepared. .... Any idea who's on-call there?"

The reg was flattered that he had asked; it made him feel more settled in the job but he still did not know the answer.

"Never mind ... I hope it's Rosni Chatterjee. Lovely girl. You'd like her."

The reg chose not to respond. It was probably just a polite remark but he was sensitive about his sexuality.

"She'll liaise with Grace and take it from there...."

There was a silence. Bill swirled his emptying cup and studied the coffee cooling in its recesses. He might have been a fortune teller looking at tea leaves.

"Poor woman" he said of Norma, wondering if she had been able to change her blouse.

Fergus Crombie was also sitting in another hospital staff room sipping coffee. It was the same sort of room as the one in which Bill and the reg were winding down with the same cheap furniture, the same mottled assortment of thank you cards pinned to the pockmarked notice board alongside out of date rotas, invocations to wash hands, the dangers of being overweight and flyers from a myriad of local takeaways who would be more than happy to deliver, any time of the day and most of the night. On the walls amidst ancient grease stains from blue tack long since defunct and posters consigned to the incinerator (before the days of recycling) were jaunty pictures of STDs and invading bacteria with accompanying advice and lots of exclamation marks. There was nothing so vulgar in the way of coffee from a vending machine however, but the altogether more refined pure-pod output of a middle of the range (so as not to seem too ostentatious) espresso machine provided by Fergus himself for the benefit of his esteemed colleagues. Mostly his esteem as it transpired, but everyone enjoyed the coffee and he was not even required to maintain a supply of the capsules. It was tacitly agreed that staff would provide their own, thereby avoiding any dissention about the less popular flavours which, like orange creams, always seemed to be the only ones left in the tin. Fergus himself liked Americano intenso - black, unsweetened, strong and a bit bitter. There had been some recent mutterings about the environmental impact of the coffee capsules: non-recyclable apparently, but the complaints had come from the right-on minority, the same people who whinged about bottled water and plastic straws in the canteen. Such small things to get waxed up about. Life was too short. Fergus always smiled, said nothing and continued to enjoy the coffee.

The room was relatively quiet which was unusual for such a large hospital, but then it was handover so most of the medics were huddled in groups over files and charts briefing each other in discreet corners and behind doors. Sorcerers, wielding stethoscopes; witches in covens practising their dark arts Fergus thought and smiled. The nurse with whom he had spent a surprisingly athletic night (there might be something in this yoga lark after all) was sitting adjacent to him, carefully avoiding his person but watching his every move. She assumed he was smiling at her and blushed, re-crossing her legs so that he had a better view of her thigh. Fergus pretended not to notice and she blushed again as he continued to smile, just the same, even as he sipped his coffee and tried to remember her name.

The door opened and a young woman stepped into the room, briskly, clearly searching for something. A comely wench Fergus thought to himself and broadened his smile. She peered around the room with a somewhat desperate air. Obviously, what she wanted was not there but perhaps if she stayed long enough it would appear, pop up from behind one of the cheap chairs or climb out from underneath the legs akimbo coffee table.

"Can I help?" *Toujours la politesse*; a damsel in distress. Sir Fergus to the rescue. He had recognised her although he could not remember her name either. No matter. She was an FY1 on surgical: a very junior doctor, qualified as a medical practitioner but very inexperienced, very new and very nervous. She was at the start of her career in the hospital and this was almost certainly her first post. All the better for him. Even if he had not already known, he would have identified her as an FYI by the way she dressed. She was still in the 'better make an effort' phase of training rather than the 'I don't give a stuff what I look like' which kicked in about halfway through FY2 and stuck until the giddy heights of Specialist Registrar began to beckon. By the time consultancy arrived she would be smart, chic and sleekly expensive. So important for private practice. She was wearing black lycra tights he noticed, with approval, the sort that had a lustre and did not sag at the knees. Her lower legs were a little too thin for his taste; the ankles were slim but the calves lacked muscle and shape. However, her upper half more than compensated for any deficiency below the knee. Above a pleasantly short skirt that closely cradled her buttocks she was wearing a fitted blouse, its long sleeves rolled up to the elbows and it was buttoned down the front. He noticed with satisfaction that the upper buttons were struggling; the collar was very open and appeared to be trying to affect an escape across her shoulders. It was intrepid, pioneering, leading the way followed steadfastly by the first four buttons of the blouse which had worked itself undone under considerable pressure from within. Her chest was on the move, straining against the fabric and squeezed into submission by one loyal button at the fifth point, grimly hanging onto its buttonhole partner. Her subsequent cleavage was deep and tight, a crevice of delight, seemingly endless, full of promise. Fergus was curious. His crotch tightened. He uncrossed his legs.

"Are you looking for something?" he asked, addressing her face. Not bad; nice hair; good skin; looks like the type to have had braces so decent teeth.

"My registrar" she replied, bereft. Yes, he was right about the teeth, Fergus congratulated himself; he usually was.

"Anything I can help with?"

She hesitated. She was desperate and she had no idea where the surgical reg had gone. Oh, why were they never there when you most needed them?

"I've a male catheterisation which needs doing now, but ... well, he's quite a big chap and I'm not sure if the catheter will reach the bladder."

"He's well endowed?"

"Yes, very."

The yoga-practising student nurse was agog.

"Suck it and see."

There was an astonished silence. Even the coffee table seemed to straighten up and pull its legs together. The FY1 flushed a deep red which, Fergus noticed, extended down her neck, over her chest and into the embrace of her fulsome cleavage which deepened to cuddle the colour.

The student nurse had begun to giggle and was noticed by the FY1 for the first time. Perhaps it was a mistake she thought, an unfortunate slip of the tongue; should she laugh too? Dr Crombie was very senior. Surely, he wouldn't have deliberately said something so...inappropriate? She flushed; frowned; fled, making sure the door was firmly shut behind her.

Ted Jones waved off his daughter from the discomfort of his wheelchair. It was quite mild for the time of year so he stayed in the doorway of his ground floor sheltered accommodation for some time after Betsy's car had moved out of view. She was driving a white Mercedes A class, as had been noted with great interest by his neighbours. A Mercedes! Aye, Ted's lass, the older one, must be doin' alreet doctorin' down south. Ted insisted that she was not down south at all but in the Midlands, having swapped Newcastle for Birmingham but as far as his neighbours were concerned (Ted came from Ireland so couldn't be expected to understand) The South consisted of anything beyond the M18 Doncaster bypass for those that drove, or York for those that did not. It was not that they minded southerners aye, but just that they were not northerners, so were much to be pitied. Still, a Mercedes. And in white! Try keeping that clean in all that Brummie smoke. Aye, she must be a canny lass.

As Betsy drove, religiously on the exact speed limit and hating those hogging the middle lane, her father receded with every passing mile to be replaced by Fergus who became ever more desirable the closer she got to Birmingham. Absence really did make the heart grow fonder. Fergus must surely have felt it too. Perhaps this was what was needed for them to take their relationship to the next level? She was ready to commit – had been for some time she now realised – but he was a free spirit. Which she loved; of course. Who wouldn't? But sometimes (just sometimes) it could be a bit unsettling. And she respected that – applauded it; rejoiced in it – an essential part of his charisma and which made life with him so unexpected and thrilling. Which, yes, she did love. Of course, she did. However, any suggestion of permanence or moving in together would, naturally, have to come from him.

"Be patient" she said sternly to Heart Radio at Wetherby and put her foot down, just for a few minutes.

Her father, meanwhile, had returned indoors and wheeled his way to the bathroom. He felt bloated and constipated. He levered himself painfully up from his seat and balanced himself precariously on his complete leg as he snatched the mirrored door of the wall cabinet open and began to rummage amongst the mess for something to make him go.

CHAPTER SIX

"It's goin' to be hardest first thing in the mornin'."

Norma stopped and Rosni Chatterjee let her visit the moment. Norma was almost a widow now. When she awoke, she would find herself alone. Suddenly sleep had become hostile, lonely and cold; the once shared bed a featureless plain of quilt and sheets and unused pillows. It had been suggested that she removed some of the pillows and slept in the middle of bed with a hot water bottle but she could not do that; not when Alan was still alive. And yes, she would interrupt whoever was trying to put her right and say that he wasn't really alive, was just being kept that way; that the real Alan had gone. She knew all that but as long as he was there, he was alive and while them machines were still working, she was sorry, pet, but no one would convince her otherwise.

Only Rosni had not contradicted her. She knew how important it was that Alan the person remained alive in Norma's mind. Ironically, it made her job easier. The concept of the living, even the partly living, giving life and relieving suffering somehow felt more real. Then death was less painful to accept as it did not seem so hopeless, so bereft, so pointless. The really difficult thing about suggesting organ donation to traumatised relatives was the timing. You could learn how to suggest it, follow as accomplished a script as you liked but, as with any really good actor, it was all about the timing. Innate. Instinctive. And like a live theatre performance you only got one shot at it. Speak too soon and you would cut off the other actors' successful delivery and ruin the drama; leave it too long and the moment would be lost, the performance destroyed. Organ opportunities did not last forever.

The two women were drinking tea, the first Rosni assumed of many cups, some with, some without biscuits for variety. She liked to let the next of kin the chance to speak first. It gave them a sense of control and her enough time to gauge her audience. Norma seemed very calm and measured which was a good sign, but could be deceptive. Like quarry lakes, still waters ran deep, concealed more and were the most dangerous. No, no sugar for her thank you pet, Norma said as it was offered and she thought of the husband's obstinate refusal to give up sugar in his tea. She was sorry now that she had ever suggested it but she had meant well. Thought it had been for the best.

"Norma?"

Silence. Had she heard? Rosni could not be sure. She tried again.

"Norma ..."

"Sorry pet. I was thinkin'..."

"Would you like to talk about it?"

Another silence. Or was it a dramatic pause?

"I want to do what's for the best." Norma put down her cup and with it, her doubts. "What Alan'd do."

Rosni also put down her cup and the two women looked at each other.

"We saw it on the telly one time, me 'n Alan. One of them hospital programmes."

A pause.

"This lass, she was in car crash and ... became like Alan ... y'know? And her Mam and Dad agreed to let the doctors have her heart for another lass who had to have it to stay alive."

"Organ donation?" Rosni offered quietly.

"Aye."

"Did you and Alan ever discuss organ donation?"

"Not really. Only the once, after that programme. I don't like the idea meself but Alan thought it was alright. He was a lovely man, y'know. Solid. Never let people down."

She was in danger of returning to the ceiling and floating away but resisted. Things to be done, pet, as Alan would have said and she did not want to let him down. But they had to be the right things. What if she got it wrong? Rosni watched the conflict on Norma's face but refrained from speaking. This was not her struggle; all she could do was watch, wait and hope. It was not as simple as just agreeing to donating the organs, she understood that. What would they take? When? Who would get 'them'? ... And what would be left of Alan afterwards? She watched as the questions followed one another in Norma's dry tortured eyes, that now needed their previous copious briny tears to sluice away and soothe her pain. So, she waited, picking up her cup again, sipping her cooling tea, unobtrusive and quiet. In Norma's time.

"Would there be somethin' left for me to bury?"

Yes. Of course, there would. Alan would look exactly the same. Rosni leaned forward to reassure as she spoke. The utmost respect and regard were shown for organ donors and their families. Funerals, cremations or whatever the family wanted took place in just the same way as if there was no organ donation. There was nothing to fear.

Norma did not seem to share her confidence but was nothing if not determined. No harm in asking was there? She had to know or how could she make the right choice? Alan would have asked and asked until he was satisfied that he had all the information he needed to make his decision – ducks in a row he had called it. When all the facts are in front then ye can work out what's best to do, he'd always said. Sometimes it had driven her mad it took that long, but he never let her down and always stuck by what he decided; always saw it through.

"Do I have to decide now?" More fear in her voice and her face.

Rosni smiled as she leaned. No, of course she didn't. Obviously sooner was better than later but there was no pressure – none whatsoever. Yes, she meant it she affirmed in response to the look of scepticism that had crept into the anguished eyes - it had to be Norma's decision and Norma's alone, after discussion with her close family of course. It had to be the right thing for her to do and she had to be sure about it. Were her family nearby? Did they know what had happened? Could she do anything to help?

"No pet, nothing. There's only me. We never had any bairns. ... We wanted them, that bad, but it didn't happen so it's just me now. It's just me to decide."

Loneliness engulfed her. Rosni felt its chilly arms enfold the small figure before her, a dishevelled little bird with damp wings and besmirched feathers, badly in need of brushing and smoothing. Downy under-feathers protruded through what had once been sleek outer plumage that now looked limp and lustreless. Skinny wrinkled fingers like chicken's feet clasped together, all knuckles and liver spots in barren fleshless prayer. I don't know what to do her body was crying out to the isolation around her, which took no notice. There's nothing left.

Norma's silent grief howled into the void.

It's all gone and I'm on my own. What do I do?

CHAPTER SEVEN

"You ask her."

"She'll only say no."

"Not if it's you."

"I wish you wouldn't say that."

"It's true though, innit? Oh, go on. You want to as much as me."

This was true and both of the Eriksson offspring knew it. Christmas was endless. I mean, like, it was okay when you opened presents and had dinner and all that stuff, but then it was Boxing Day and you had to stay in with The Family. Gross. Boring. The whole house was grossed out with relatives banging on about what they used to do, and wanting to know about school, and what you were planning to do in the future. Plus, they had to share a room which really sucked. And wasn't it illegal for a girl and a boy to share at their age, even for a short time (not short enough) while everyone stayed? Not that She ever listened and even if She did, it made no difference, because She was always right, even when She was wrong. At least now the relatives had gone, they were back in their own rooms and New Year's Eve was over. Which had been awful, even worse than usual. Why did they have to have a mother like Her? Everyone else had been allowed to meet their mates and have a good time. Birmingham rocked on New Year's Eve, but oh no, not them. She'd insisted that they stay in and they see the New Year in 'as a family'. Yeah, they knew Dad was ill – their lives revolved around it and it sucked, 'specially for him – but even he'd said they could go out and have a good time. He was great like that. He never made a fuss about anything but She wasn't having any of it. Never did.

"We can get a bus" the elder brother offered.

"I'll walk".

Archie Eriksson laughed out loud. I mean there was desperate and 'desperate' and his younger sister never walked anywhere. Not in those shoes anyway. Siobhan smirked, slyly. She wouldn't have to if he asked Mum in the right way; it always worked. What was he waiting for? They could say they wanted to get Dad a birthday present... Yeah, alright, so it's not until the end of the month but if you tell her I've got exams and I'll be revising she's bound to say yes.

Oh alright. Archie said he would do it but she'd have to buy him lunch – a Big Mac? Yeah, yeah, whatever. Just do it and then they could go to the sales like everyone else in Birmingham. Anything to get out of the house and have a laugh. To be normal. Siobhan would even pay his bus fare. She might be younger, but she understood money.

Also heading in the direction of the sales but with no intention of stopping there and buying anything was Professor Phoebe Dennington. To reach the hospital from her side of Birmingham she would have to run the gauntlet of the sales traffic – where did it all come from? What was wrong with these people? Didn't they have anything better to do than play homage to Mammon? Weren't the excesses of Christmas enough? They were in her way and she had to get to work. And why choose New Year's Day to go bargain hunting when it was all that anyone seemed to have been doing since Boxing Day? She thought that the Festive Season (whatever that meant) was all about family gatherings and spending quality time with loved ones. Not for her of course, she had been working; on-call over the whole period which not only earned her the gratitude of her more domesticated colleagues but gave her the satisfaction of being legitimately busy enough to avoid her sister with her odious offspring, who were just at that most irritating puberty stage. God knows, she encountered enough hormonal youth through her work at the hospital and it was always a relief to have them put under. In her experience, the only acceptable teenager was an unconscious one.

Really, this traffic was ridiculous. Birmingham was getting worse.

In Newcastle it was similar but enlivened with the onslaught of remorseless rain. Traffic staggered and laced its way around the city centre, a metal corset tightening and squeezing the breath out of the city's lungs which became wet and heavy. Rosni and Norma watched the rain trying to break into the sanctuary of their quiet room and then fall back, defeated, crying itself out against the windows. It was day, but seemed like night. Nothing had been said for a long time. Rosni knew when not to speak.

"I think it's what Alan'd want."

Norma shattered the silence and it broke apart. Neither it nor Rosni were ready and it came as a surprise, unexpected and exceptionally loud. Even the rain seemed to be listening. Yet, still Rosni did not speak.

"Aye. It is."

"You're giving your consent, Norma?"

"I am."

"To donating Alan's organs?"

"Yes."

For the first time Norma now looked at Rosni not as the lass with the tea and kind words but as a Specialist Nurse in Organ Donation.

"You'll have to tell me what to do."

That was the easy part Rosni said; the really difficult bit was over and Norma was wonderful. Her decision meant life – proper quality of life – and a future for the recipients who would almost certainly otherwise die. Organs were so valuable and in such high demand. What Norma had done was not just generous but life saving and, in a meaningful way, Alan would live on through the new life he was giving to others. There was nothing Norma needed to worry about. As a SNOD (yes, wasn't it a dreadful thing to be known as? Even Norma smiled) Rosni would liaise with another organ donation specialist nurse and together they would guide the new widow through the donation process, every step of the way.

Norma looked bereft. What was the matter? Rosni wondered for one moment if she had changed her mind – it often happened. Once the reality of the decision to donate became action people panicked and retreated; it was all suddenly more than an idea and the recognition that the body of their beloved was to be dissected and distributed among others was too frightening, too horrible to contemplate. But she had underestimated Norma. No, she had not changed her mind. Alan would've stuck with it – he could be that stubborn. So she would too. It was just that she liked Rosni and had got used to her. Why couldn't she be the one to accompany her on this journey? Did there have to be someone else who was no doubt lovely but ... a stranger?

Yes, for Norma's sake it did.

At this point Rosni took Norma's hands in her own and held them, tight. Another set of hands leaching the sorrow and pain of someone else into themselves, anchoring Norma to the earth when all she wanted to do was float, far away.

There had to be another SNOD as well as a Rosni so that Norma had the comfort of knowing that she could change her mind if she wanted, without guilt or embarrassment and that there would always be more than one person to travel with her. Rosni would be there too but her colleague would take care of everything. The three of them would meet and Norma would get to know her, and yes, she would be lovely and no longer a stranger. Whatever happened, Norma was not alone. Nor would she be, at any stage. What she was doing was wonderful: generous and brave. Alan would be so proud of her.

"I hope so, pet. But it's not being generous y'know. I'm bein' selfish. I'm makin' sure there'll always be a bit Alan in the world."

Phoebe Dennington was in the car when the call came. Her mobile rang just as she was managing to get past a bus that was pulling away from a stop. Really, why couldn't they wait? She had to put her foot down halfway through the manoeuvre and swing out almost into the middle of the road as the bus resumed its place in the traffic flow after indicating its intention for what, less than a few seconds? It was absolutely reckless driving and in other circumstances she would have reported it but her phone was ringing with what would almost certainly be an important call. She accelerated past the bus, ignoring the unnecessarily crude gesture the driver threw at her (Philistine) and roared forward to the traffic lights which were now on red. Bugger. Birmingham had the slowest traffic lights in the world. Honestly, it was if someone had deliberately set them at slow to death just out of ignorance and spite. Some petty bureaucrat somewhere without any concept of pace or urgency. Not for the first time she speculated about the possibility of senior hospital personnel having carte blanche access to bus and taxi lanes when journeying to work. What was the point of letting ambulances through if when they got to their destination there were no senior medics to make decisions about their occupants? She was just as important as any emergency vehicle and should be treated accordingly. However, the light was red so she would just be able to identify the caller and pick up any message. No one could possibly object; she was a doctor. No, not just a doctor. A surgeon. A senior consultant.

It was from Ann Williams, the Liver Recipient Coordinator. A donor organ had become available. Could they speak asap please? She did not need to say that time was of the essence – Phoebe used that phrase as if she had invented it.

Phoebe felt a thrill. Her whole body flushed with pleasure and she was the first away from the lights when they changed to green. Fortunately, she was now passing the shopping mall and the roads were clearing. And she wasn't just a senior Consultant Liver Surgeon; she was a Professor at a Centre of Excellence. She swung into the staff car park and lamented again that such senior medics did not have designated parking places alongside those of the most senior managers, the Medical Director and Chairman of the Hospital Trust. Obviously, it would not be appropriate for every consultant; some were quite junior and had yet to prove themselves but she was an accredited, internationally published consultant of some standing with a reputation to maintain. Surely it could not be right that she had to share precious and often limited parking facilities with every other member of staff? Most of who worked in a lesser capacity, like the kitchen or the pharmacy. Important yes – team work was so important – but not critical.

Spinning the steering wheel with the palm of one hand as if she was polishing a window, the way she had seen it done on TV motoring programmes. she curled her Range Rover into an empty slot with an agility surprising for such a cumbersome beast. Of course she would not normally drive such a large 4 x 4 but her position demanded it. Who knew when and in what conditions she might be required to drive? A reliable all-weather vehicle was a necessity, not to mention the security angle. Birmingham was not the city it once was; areas of it were completely no go, not that she ever went, but a woman alone in a car could never take chances. That was why she always kept her phone within easy reach on the front passenger seat but her briefcase out of sight. At night she always waited until she had arrived and was within hospital premises before putting on her earrings.

Even as the car engine was being shut off, she was reaching for her mobile and hitting the return call facility. There was no answer which was annoying so she in turn left a message. Ann was one of the more efficient LRCs so ought to get back to her in a timely fashion. Nevertheless, no time to waste.

Walking along the unusually quiet corridor, kitten heels mewing painfully as they impaled the hard floor, she noted that there had been no response to her most recent tweets. Twitter was an occupational hazard, like all social media but had its uses, especially in the art of self-promotion she had noticed with disapproval. Too many of her colleagues simply used it as a platform for their own self-serving glorification rather than as a tool for information and education as she did. Theirs was a teaching hospital, affiliated to the university. Students were advised to follow senior members of staff who posted pertinent medical news and information, links to papers, recommendations for further study, advice and guidance. How disappointing it was that there was so little uptake. But the calibre of students was not what it was. It would be necessary to talk to the Medical School again.

"Morning Professor Dennington. Happy New Year!" The voice was warm, the body Amazonian, the shoes flat and well-worn and all belonged to Ann Williams.

"Good morning. Happy New Year to you too. Did you get my message?"

Ann waved her mobile cheerfully in the air. She was at least eighteen inches taller than Phoebe who resented having to look up at her. The woman was one of those odd beings who was well built and sturdy but not fat. Big boned Phoebe's mother would have called it. Ann was athletic in a jolly hockey sticks kind of way and Phoebe would not have been surprised if she played on a netball team, or even lacrosse (she had been to that kind of school). Or swimming. She could imagine Ann thrashing through cold water doing butterfly stroke or backstroke, all quivering flesh, flexed muscles and vigorous splashing. She and Ann were probably about the same age – late forties, early fifties she guessed but looking at Ann it was hard to reconcile their respective images. One so hearty and overstated, with untidy hair and no make-up. The other sophisticated, and, if she said so herself, an exquisitely balanced combination of elegance and professionalism.

"So we have a donor liver?"

"We do. In Newcastle. What a great way to start the New Year for someone! A complete game changer."

"Let's find out what condition it's in first."

Ann's enthusiasm survived intact but she knew better than to argue so merely nodded, apparently in agreement. Once the condition of the organ had been established, they would then be able to select an appropriate recipient. There was a long list from which to choose; so few organs; so many who needed transplants.

"Top of the list?" Ann asked. Theoretically that was how the allocation worked but usually it did not follow. Time spent on the list rarely equated to a potential recipient's degree of urgency and suitability of the available liver. Everything depended on the organ-recipient match. They had nearly reached the double doors at the end of the corridor. Ann stepped forward and pushed one open to let Phoebe pass; the mewling kitten heels never so much as broke purr as they clipped their way to the lift. Phoebe's office was on hallowed higher ground, three floors up. Ann worked at ground level. However, she too waited outside the lift; clearly the conversation was not over.

"I hope so." Phoebe replied, nodding graciously, as much acknowledgement of Ann's door opening as was required. "Who is it?"

"Graham Eriksson. Autoimmune disease of the liver. Primary biliary cirrhosis."

"Don't you mean cholangitis?" Phoebe was severe. "Cirrhosis is only a feature of advanced disease so the name was changed in 2014 to primary biliary cholangitis. I was involved in that decision. It's still known as PBC though."

'Although you should know better' reeked the air, but Ann took no notice. She was used to Phoebe Dennington.

"Do I know him?"

'You should' Ann's expression said as she spoke,

"Tall, ex-rugby player, accommodating. A man of few words. ... Clearly you haven't met his wife. No one forgets Heather Eriksson."

Fergus was at home when Betsy called. It was his landline, the number for which only very few knew and which he never answered. He could not understand why the woman had not called his mobile like everyone else; she knew he would not pick up but then, as he thought about it, maybe that was exactly why she had done it. He was being reminded that she was one of the exclusive *coterie* who had access to his number. Phoebe never rang his landline though.

He pictured the two women. Both slim, successful, intelligent and ambitious. He really quite liked them. Phoebe was more established financially and emotionally – self-contained and measured. She could be calculating and was by nature mathematical which was odd because that's what you would have expected from the anaesthetist. Betsy was more emotional and dependent; she needed to be needed which was less appealing but on the plus side made her more sexually adventurous and less inhibited. Definitely more fun in that department. He might try some of those recently acquired yoga moves with her. Phoebe was more conservative and preferred it in the bedroom but what she lacked in originality was more than compensated for by her stamina and persistence; sex was a skill, like surgery or learning a language that had to be mastered. She would practice until she was word perfect and he was more than happy to assist. Besides, she made no emotional demands which kept him intrigued. That they all worked together in the same hospital was very convenient and created an added frisson certainly to his life; neither knew about his relationship with the other and that suited him just fine. It was not the military action he had so loved in the Marines but was better than nothing and at least he had the adrenaline rush of the air ambulance and being a paramedic to get him away from the confines of the hospital. Otherwise he would suffocate.

His mobile rang. It was Betsy. He let it ring then go to voicemail. It had been a busy night and he wanted to sleep.

In her office Phoebe was giving her keyboard hell. She keyed very fast and devastatingly accurately – a skill she had perfected over a comparatively short time by constant practice to music with a regular and pronounced rhythm. Now she plied the keys with pace and consistency; such an asset when there was so much NHS paperwork. That made her smile, but only to herself. How typical of the NHS to continue calling it paperwork but (here her smile disappeared into her throat) there were still ludicrous amounts of paper/hard copies and files that still had to be generated. Letters of appointment and follow up reports were still being sent to patients, GPs and God alone knew who else. Then letters confirming already-sent appointment letters or changes of appointment... the time! The cost! She sucked her lips into creases as if swallowing quinine but then remembered her lipstick, so eased them back into shape. And all the time playing her keyboard with perfect pitch and pace.

Her mobile shrilled and shivered on the desk.

"Professor Phoebe Dennington" she informed it as she played the computer keyboard with one hand. It was Ann. The consultant was irritated. What could the woman possibly want now? As the senior operating surgeon, she, Phoebe, had given the go ahead to accept the donor liver. Newcastle had been anxious to begin the retrieval process which even now was underway. The donor had had treatment withdrawn which was very sad - devastating - for his family of course, but life had to go on and no one understood that better than a transplant surgeon such as herself. Phoebe felt sympathy for the unknown family – who wouldn't? – but her primary concern was for the patient to whom she could restore a future. It was important to remember the positive aspect of the process when retrieving organs.

"Yes?" She tried not to sound peeved.

There was a problem. Organ retrieval and analysis completed, the report on the donor liver had just come through and Ann had been reading it. Yes, and the problem was? Phoebe interjected; get to the point, Ann. Time is of the essence.

"The condition of the liver."

"Go on."

"Our donor was a smoker and a drinker; BMI 39 so the liver is fatty. Graham Eriksson's a big man so we have a physical match but I don't know how secure the surgical outcome might be." Phoebe was about to interject but Ann cut her off at the pass, "Obviously that's beyond my remit."

Indeed it is Phoebe silently agreed.

"The organ is a DCD and therefore marginal which will have to be fully explained to any potential recipient" Ann continued then stopped; left it hanging. Over to you Professor D. Here we go Ann thought and braced herself.

"You've spoken to the Newcastle SNOD?"

"Not yet." Ann just knew that somehow; she would be under suspicion. "I wanted your input first."

“Quite right.”

Ann smiled. Phoebe Dennington was so predictable. Her obsession with protocol and status would have been amusing if it wasn’t so aggressive.

“I shall discuss it with the Medical Director, Professor Hugh Goldberg who’s a hepatologist and on-call today“ Phoebe announced.

I know who the MD is Ann was thinking, and what he specialises in, thanks. But said nothing.

Phoebe continued.

“I suggest that, initially, we go with Graham Eriksson as arranged. He’s been waiting a long time and is physiologically suitable. Get all the background from the SNOD and let me know how you get on.”

The call was over; Phoebe was already cutting Ann off and returning to her keyboard even as Ann was telling her that yes, she would and that she would be touch as soon as she could. It was a good thing that she was alone in her office so no one saw her click her heels and salute the wall.

CHAPTER EIGHT

She had done it. And survived. The alarm had gone off, she was awake and had actually slept quite well. All through the night. Norma lay on her side of the bed and felt the hot water bottle at her knees where it had slipped during the night after she had fallen asleep clutching it against her belly. She was lying on her side, just as she always did but knew that when she turned onto her back everything would be different. So she lay as she was, gazing at the bedside table, the lamp, the beaker of water, her glasses and the old-fashioned alarm clock in the leather travelling case that had been a present from Alan many, many years ago. Not that they ever really travelled, but it was always useful he'd said, in case they did. And he was right – like that time they'd gone on a coach tour to the Scottish Highlands and had to be up betimes for breakfast in the guest houses and once, even a hotel. Didn't want to oversleep and miss the full English Alan had said. Bless him, she thought. He'd loved a proper fried breakfast with a bit black puddin'. The hotel was very swish and the lass in reception had offered to give them a wake-up call in their room but they had refused. Didn't want to be a bother and anyway, they had their own alarm clock with them which would do the job just champion.

She was going to have to turn over. Lie on her back, face the emptiness, feel the space. It was still dark but not cold: the central heating had chattered and tutted into action as usual, just as if Alan was still there. But he wasn't. She knew because she had seen him in the chapel of rest at the hospital, so still and quiet, his eyes closed and all sealed up. He was washed and dressed in one of those hospital gowns and lay under a beautifully laundered sheet, still with its fold creases, as white and carefully ironed as anything she could do. It was strange to see him like that and not snoring or making gurgly noises in his throat as he slept, or seeing his chest moving up and down below the soft cotton pyjama top with the stripes that went all skew whiff down the front where the buttons pulled. His pyjamas! Without thinking she levered herself completely over onto her other side and thrust her arm under the plumped-up pillows beside her own. Yes! They were there. His pyjamas. Neatly folded by herself and put there for when they came home after seeing in the New Year at the pub. A lifetime ago.

She was not going to cry. Alan would not want that; he hated seeing people cry, especially a woman. Instead she sat up and removed her nightdress swiftly, in one movement, over the top of her head and flung it to the floor. Then she put on his pyjama jacket. It was huge: far too big and the sleeves hung over her hands as if trying to reach down to pick up the discarded nightdress. No matter. She rolled up the sleeves and stood up on the bed. It was a bit wobbly but she kept her balance as she slid one leg and then the other into the trousers which draped themselves over her feet like running water. She tied the stretched string firmly around her waist so that they were secure then sat down, rolled up the bottoms of the trouser legs and got out of bed. Went downstairs, put on the kettle and picked up her life.

She wore them all day, that night and much of the following day. Then she took them off and put them back under the pillow on the bed they still shared and never washed them again.

"You're not going out and that's final. You went shopping yesterday. I won't tell you again."

Heather had spoken and in the kind of tone that both Archie and Siobhan knew only too well: that no room for manoeuvre or negotiation tone that signalled a complete impasse. It was pointless to argue; she wouldn't listen anyway. The reasoning that it was nearly the end of the Christmas holidays so they should be at home was so obscure, so redolent of their mother that they had learned when to give up, give in and speak only to mutter under their breath while posting f*** -laden anti-authority messages on social media. Heather, they knew, would never see them but still neither of them actually liked to write out forbidden language in full. Also, it endowed them with an irreproachable but anarchic virtual street cred which was really cool but which was beginning to bore their Fb friends.

They were in the kitchen. Dad was still in bed, having a not so good day. Too many late nights Heather had diagnosed with the piety of the righteous; she had told him not to wait up and see in the new year but, of course, he would insist that he knew best and now he was paying for it. Thank goodness she had absolutely and categorically refused to allow alcohol of any description for the occasion. Such a ridiculous concept; she had never understood the obsession for over indulgence as a form of celebration. Anyway, Graham's condition precluded any such insanity. Siobhan and Archie would benefit she had reminded them, again, both by example and practice. Besides, they were too young to drink; under age; it was against the law and in this instance - but only this occasion mark you - she agreed with the law of the land. Siobhan threw her brother a look. Here we go again it said and they mutually agreed to retreat, in silence, metaphorically crawling from the room backwards on hands and knees but still managing to switch the radio station from Four to One as they departed.

Heather never even looked around as she repaired the damage and restored Radio Four. One petty act of adolescent rebellion did not a battle make and she always rose above such things. It was a point of principle. F*** the principal Archie had written on Facebook until one of his more erudite schoolmates had put him right.

If Heather knew that her offspring had left the room it made no difference. Her voice carried. She wanted a progress report on Archie's English coursework. It had to be read through and checked by the end of the day and she was busy, there was always so much more to do than the children ever appreciated. Really, they had no idea how lucky they were. She would make time to have a good look at his text and make any observations and/or corrections so that Archie would be able to complete another draft before he went to bed. Which draft was this? She couldn't remember. Three or four? Reply came there none so she continued, undeterred, as she made her husband's breakfast, loaded the dishwasher and delivered a homily on the benefits of doing a core subject GSCE a year early. Get English out of the way then focus on other subjects which were more demanding and more interesting. Everybody spoke their own language so reading and writing it were merely a formality; get thee behind and then concentrate on maths and sciences which were so much more relevant. She had never understood the obsession (another one) of the educational establishment with English, especially literature. What was the point?

Siobhan had disappeared up to her room, once more her own, and was contemplating footwear. As usual, Heather seemed not to have noticed. Siobhan rarely featured above the family parapet much to Archie's disgust. It wasn't fair. He didn't ask to be born first. Now Heather had moved on from coursework and was considering the more pressing issue of hot beverage choices.

"Archie, go and see if your father wants tea or coffee. Tell him there's no toast; he's on a diet."

It ought to be tea she was telling herself. One always has tea first but it's getting on for mid-morning so he might want coffee and I'd better let him decide, although he's definitely not having any carbohydrates, whatever he says. Throughout the whole of this exchange Heather had not turned around once. It did not matter, Archie would hear and obey, whether he liked it or not. However just as he was about to begin his mission of mercy in point of caffeine the phone rang, in the hall, well within Heather's aegis.

"Get the phone Archie please ... now."

Uttering profanities and gesticulating lewdly in his head, her first born directed himself towards the call of the landline, outraged and perplexed as to why anyone chose to ring such a contraption when everyone had mobiles, even his mother, not that she ever turned it on. Heather removed her head from the recesses of the dishwasher and tried to hear what was being said. Her son was developing too much of a Brummie accent she decided as he spoke – acceptable enough perhaps at school and with his peers but inappropriate for the kind of future she envisaged for him. He needed to develop a telephone voice in the first instance and they could build on that. Traces of an accent were a sign of warmth and cultural ownership – they even had them on the BBC these days – but one did not want to be defined by one's regional origins.

"It's for Dad" came the unacceptable Birmingham-edged accent from the hall.

"I'll take it" replied the displaced edges-rubbed-off boarding school drawl and Heather followed her voice to take possession of the receiver.

"Heather Eriksson here, wife of Graham. ... Oh, hello Ann. He's not available at the moment I'm afraid. Can I help? ... That sounds like good news. We'll come in and discuss it straightaway. I just need to find someone to watch the children then we should be with you in a couple of hours."

In her office on the ground floor Ann Williams put down the phone and shook her head, whether in dismay, disbelief or amusement it was hard to say. Weren't the Eriksson children teenagers? The eldest, a boy, must be 14 or 15 at least.

In Newcastle it began to look as if the rain would never stop. Norma was still wearing Alan's pyjamas and had kept the curtains half closed at the windows of the sturdy stone terraced house in North Shields where they had lived all their married life. We'll stay put, pet, Alan had said when it became apparent that they were not going to be parents. It's not as if they needed the space; they were close to the Yards and the shops and it was where they had grown up. No bairns, no need to move. Norma would have liked a bit garden so Alan had built her a couple of window boxes, one for the front window and one for the kitchen at the back that had originally been a scullery but which had been extended out under a flat roof, nearly all the way to the stone wall separating them from the back alley. The kitchen had been built using money inherited from Alan's parents when their house, in the same street had been sold for an astonishing amount of money. Who'd a thought it? And it had even had a downstairs bathroom. Sadly, the window box at the front had had to be removed as the youth of North Shields experienced teenage angst, the only remedy for which appeared to be the destruction either by violence or urination of anything that grew within its wooden dimensions. Now it lay on the ground beneath its kitchen counterpart, barren and alone. Norma knew how it felt.

Half a mile away on the other side of the scrubby park with the outline of the once glorious Victorian bandstand etched on the concrete-covered flag stones, Ted Jones was also indoors, not so much avoiding the rain as unaware of it. He seemed to have spent the last day in the bathroom. Thank God it was inside and not the netty of his youth he mused as he perched on the toilet seat, good foot on the floor, knee stump prone, pointing to the door as if to show the way out in case its owner had got lost. Not lost, just stuck Ted thought. Perhaps he had overdone the laxative. Now he could not only 'go', he could not bloody stop. Bring back the constipation he groaned as he bent forward to ease his discomfort. He pressed his good foot against the lino floor and pushed for greater purchase while his stump tensed and did its best to help – with you in spirit it seemed to be saying.

A groan of relief and he decided to risk it; he'd get himself back together and venture out to the kitchenette for a cup of tea. That always helped. Balancing with one arm against the wall he pulled himself up and began the process of wiping and dressing. Then he stood up, hopped, steadied himself and turned to flush. Feck. There was blood in the toilet bowl. On the seat, the lid and even on the wall. Lots of it. Bright red. Brash. Unmistakeable.

The Erikssons had arrived and were being entertained by Ann Williams in her office, which Heather seemed to fill. No, no coffee thank you; they would rather like to get on with things. Where was Professor Dennington? Heather hoped she would be there very soon. She and Graham were always punctual, on principle. She looked meaningfully at her watch and then at the clock on the wall as she spoke. Ann heartily wished she would have a biscuit or something sweet.

"Professor Dennington will be here any second" she crooned. "Did you manage to find someone to look after the children?" Be bright and engaging; create a diversion; keep them talking. Where the hell is Phoebe?

"My mother" Heather barked, as if it was a disease. "Fortunately she lives nearby and is retired" so available at all times was the implication, and happy to oblige which is useful and where exactly is Professor Dennington? She was now glaring at the closed door. It worked. No knock or even a tap and the door opened to admit the missing professor who smiled carefully and entered the room as on a catwalk. No need for introductions she seemed to say; you must know who I am.

"Hello everyone. Well, this is good news isn't it?" She smiled ever so slightly more and sat down on the empty chair that awaited her.

To general surprise, Graham spoke.

Only to say, "Hello" admittedly, but he felt he should. They had met before, in clinic, albeit a while back but he felt he knew her.

Heather did not. She held out her hand.

"Heather Eriksson" she announced as the hand made to shake one of Phoebe's, which gasped with the strength of the greeting. "We haven't met. Are you a senior consultant? I Googled you but it didn't say. Your professorship is from somewhere in Australia, is that right?"

Ann dared not look at her erudite colleague who was still smiling, radiating malevolence. However, the lesser mortal who only had an office on the ground floor, was listening avidly; there had been so much speculation about Phoebe's credentials, all of it unresolved. Ooh this would be good in the canteen later ... and lunch (here she too glanced at her watch) was not far off. She tried not to smile.

"Coolangatta University, Queensland" Phoebe replied somewhat abruptly. Ann made a mental note and wondered how it was spelt. But Heather had other fish to fry.

"Never heard of it" she sniffed and went straight for the jugular. "Tell us about the donor please."

Ann replied with enthusiasm. It was a relief to be able to talk and smile legitimately. "Anonymous, obviously. Male, sixty years old, married, no children. He died from a cardiac arrest on New Year's Eve."

Graham's head bowed both in sorrow and silent gratitude. Heather wanted to know more.

"Otherwise healthy?" she spoke like a shotgun. Ann ceased smiling and went for it.

"He was a smoker, overweight with high blood pressure and

type 2 diabetes but no other previous recorded illnesses so yes, healthy enough. He's also a match in height and build for you, Graham." If she had hoped to deflect the wife by addressing the husband she failed and was already regretting her use of 'enough'. Heather would not like that and, to be fair, she might have a point.

"A smoker? Oh dear. How overweight?"

You had to hand it to her, Heather asked all the most pertinent questions; she seemed to have a nose for it.

"Body Mass Index of 39."

The number hung in the air, soft mist descending. Ann felt it fall and shroud expectation. Heather looked at her husband who looked at his feet, as if they would speak for him.

"Quite overweight then?" Heather carved a path through the mist straight to the point. It was a rhetorical question to which they all knew answer. However, Heather was not one to leave anything to doubt. "Bordering on obese" she added, regarding Ann with a critical eye. Phoebe was slender and probably athletic so nothing to disapprove of there. Graham was contained if not exactly trim but would pass muster. Heather herself observed a strict regime of high protein, high fibre, low carbohydrate fare, organic wherever possible. Enlightened pescatarianism was her mantra and her husband had benefitted. It had been such a problem when he was obliged to give up rugby and had all that muscle to shift before it turned to fat but the loss of the club, beer and post-match excesses was no loss at all now that his illness precluded boisterous exercise and over-indulgence. Always a silver lining, that was her guiding principle. It was so important to accentuate the positive. Nevertheless.

"What is the liver like?"

Her question was directed at Ann but she was looking at Phoebe. As was the Liver Recipient Coordinator herself; even Graham and his feet appeared to be awaiting a response from the professor in their midst, she of the ultimate say so. Phoebe however was intently studying an obviously important document in the slim file on her lap which she had removed from her briefcase at the start of the meeting. Perhaps the answer was in there? If so, she was saying nothing. Ann uncrossed her legs, planted her size nines on the floor then changed her mind and re-crossed her legs the other way round. The silence was liquid, threatening to drown them so Ann – Why me? Why do I do it? - picked up the reins of the discussion and tackled the issue.

The liver was moderately fatty, at very least. The donor had suffered two cardiac arrests as a result of which there had been enough downtime to deprive the brain of oxygen. Although he was not brain stem dead, a decision had been made that further treatment was futile and as a result, the difficult decision had been made to withdraw support. It was such a tragedy for him and for his family as she was sure they would understand. They did; of course they did. Heather nodded sympathetically. Graham focussed even harder on his feet which seemed to offer their condolences. Phoebe studied her document. After a brief moment of respectful silence, Ann continued.

"This means that the liver comes from what is known as a DCD donor ... which does make it more marginal."

"Marginal?"

"A what?"

Husband and wife spoke together, united but only for the briefest of moments. Heather shot her other half down with a look that caught him right between the eyes. He muttered something that sounded like an apology and resumed the rapport with the occupants of his shoes. Ann chose to answer the husband – he was after all, the potential recipient. It was his body; he had a right to know. And she did not like Heather.

"A DCD" she repeated. "Donation after circulatory death, when death is the result of treatment withdrawal and the turning off ventilatory support or similar machinery at the time when the donor organs are ready to be removed." If Graham heard, let alone understood, he gave not the slightest clue.

"Marginal you say? Is it safe? What are the risks?" Nothing and no one, especially the oversized likes of Ann was going to deter Heather in her quest for knowledge and precise answers. What an awesome interviewer she would have made; motherhood was wasted on her Phoebe thought as she turned her attention to a new document which she briefly surveyed before closing the file. Her moment had come; as she closed the file, she presented herself to her audience.

"Let me answer that" she announced as if Ann had prevented her from speaking and she was now having to barge her way into the debate. Ann suppressed the urge to slap her and, taking her cue from the redoubtable Graham, now studied her own feet while he abandoned his to gaze at Phoebe. Taking her time, calm, measured and consummately reassuring, Phoebe had switched into her most 'trust me, I'm the expert' mode and began to explain. No transplant was 100% guaranteed, the Erikssons knew that; they had always known it. There were always risks associated with any transplant but she ...

Mrs Eriksson also resisted – just – the urge to slap the professor and interrupted. Phoebe was shocked. The rudeness of the woman! She was not accustomed to people cutting in on her conversations, especially during medical consultations. However, she would always be professional so she smiled, so tightly that her lips became a lipstick line. Besides, there was no diverting Heather in full spate. The woman was a torrent

"We know that" the cloudburst was saying. "Just tell us what the risks are in this case. We don't like the sound of marginal."

A brief respite, the deluge stopped and Phoebe realised that she was being permitted to speak. Picking up a particularly sharp-edged tone she thrust at her opponent and struck her a warning slash across the torso, where it would not show.

"Increased risk of initial poor function after transplant; primary dysfunction; delayed graft function or, in extremis, early graft failure and patient survival. There is also the increased risk of previously undiagnosed malignancy in a liver from a donor of this age." So, now you know. Suck it up. Bitch. What she did not say was that the risks could be reduced by minimising the time the organ spent out of the body – the cold ischaemic time. Ann was shocked and only just prevented herself from mouthing cold ischaemic at Phoebe, whose face was as frigid as any retrieved organ on ice. Perhaps, Ann thought, she's coming to that.

Ann's office was beginning to resemble an arena where gladiatorial combat to the death appeared to be the next item on the agenda so she too abandoned communication with her footwear and flew, as it were, with winged heels to the rescue. Wearing conciliation and peace as protective clothing she flung herself into the fray to defuse the conflict. With the tone of a nanny comforting irascible children and huge satisfaction she outflanked Phoebe. It was important that the Erikssons knew the full details about any risks, of course it was. That was their right and the transplant unit would be failing in their duty of care if they were not completely open and transparent. It was Graham's body (heavy emphasis on Graham) and had to be his decision. An informed decision – there could be no other. However, and here she outflanked Heather who was about to speak (also very satisfying), it was important that the risks were offset against Graham's progressive autoimmune disease. Without a transplant there would never be any improvement in his condition, which, unfortunately, would only deteriorate further. He could only expect more of his current symptoms – increasing tiredness, lethargy and the itching would only get worse before further deterioration set in. Graham squirmed. The itching! Already intolerable it ate him up, gnawed him into a frenzy. He scratched the top of his legs and the small of his back, his default setting before clenching his fists to mentally punch it into submission. Don't think about it Heather said. What the hell did she know?

But there was more. Wasn't there always? Graham thought. Apparently, he could look forward to developing ascites where his abdomen would fill with fluid which would cause unpleasant discomfort (tell him about it) and shortness of breath before further complications set in: bacterial peritonitis, haemorrhaging blood vessels, increased encephalopathy (as if he wasn't confused and discombobulated enough as his brain struggled to cope with all the changes in his body), coma, a ventilator and then death. There was a silence when, finally, Ann finished. Graham was once more in deep communication with his feet and the floor so no one saw the incipient leakage in his eyes. But he would not cry. Not here. In fact, when Ann resumed her oration, he wanted to laugh but the bitter taste in his mouth gagged it at inception.

What was encouraging she said, too brightly, was that the risks were reduced where transplant took place in a stable patient, such as Graham at the moment ... although that might not be the case in the future.

Ann was on a roll. Graham seemed to be taking it quite well, considering. She had their attention; this was her comfort zone, well outside Phoebe Dennington. Time to follow up the emotive with the factual then let them get on with it; out of her hands but even the professor would not be able to find fault with her performance.

It might interest them to know that there had been a substantial increase in successful transplants of such marginal organs in recent years – 584 last year alone. Yes, she was sure of her facts; Professor Dennington was welcome to see the documentation and the Erikssons too if they wished. As the Recipient Co Ordinator she would like to suggest that this was an opportunity not to be missed. There was, as they knew only too well, such a severe shortage of donor livers that there was no saying when another one would be available, never mind one that was such an excellent match to Graham physically. Dramatic pause. Point made. Wait a second then throw it over to them. It was entirely the Eriksson's decision; theirs and theirs alone although she and Professor Dennington (she ignored Phoebe) would do anything they could to help. Of course.

Now Heather took the floor, including that from under her husband's feet. Yes, it was their decision. And that decision would be based on what they considered best for them. Graham had his family to consider – not just his wife but also two vulnerable, children who needed their father. The children were highly sensitive, a little highly strung in the case of Archie, the elder who was on the Autistic Spectrum. His sister was more grounded but suffered from a debilitating wheat intolerance which left her susceptible to infection and affected her self-esteem.

Phoebe was intrigued. "How?" Perhaps this was an opportunity for a research paper to which she could put her name.

"She does not like being different. The psychological effects of a special diet are profound on the self-image of an impressionable young girl. Eating disorders are a constant worry; Siobhan needs the guidance of a father and a male role model to help her cope."

Everyone looked at the role model who was now studying his clenched fists. Eventually, Phoebe surmised, he might even look up. Meanwhile Ann was considering Archie. Had he been diagnosed as Autistic? Heather would know, it went without saying, that everyone was on the spectrum somewhere but was Archie very high on the scale?

Heather flamed with pride. She would not allow her son to be labelled so had refused to have him formally assessed; it was a point of principle with her, and Graham. Archie was an extremely intelligent, sensitive young man who required careful nurturing. He did not respond well to change and exhibited many of the characteristics of those with Autism – intellectual, obsessive with limited social awareness. He was undoubtably gifted at maths and physics; there was nothing he did not understand. His teachers were incompetent and completely failed to recognise his talents while the other pupils felt threatened by his superior intellect. No one understood him outside the immediate family. They were considering home schooling him, which she would undertake as she was so close to him emotionally but in the interests of balance, Graham was essential as a figure of authority and example. Archie's symptoms of OCD had been more noticeable of late and she was convinced it was linked to the emotional trauma he was experiencing as a result of their father's illness. Archie, even more than his sister, needed both parents.

Seizing the brief interlude which followed in which Heather was required to breathe, Ann leapt in to try and regain the ascendant. 'Both parents' was exactly what they were trying to achieve with the proposed transplant and, here she avoided Phoebe's gimlet gaze, she explained about the benefit of a prompt decision in terms of the cold ischaemic time.

To the general astonishment of the assembled company, including himself, Graham found that he was speaking. Fists clenched to resist the temptation to scratch he had at last looked up and was addressing Ann and Phoebe.

"I want what's best for my family" he said, then looked at Heather who nodded approval and took one of his hands in her own.

"Graham and I need to discuss this in private ... When do you need our decision?

"As soon as possible. Within the hour?" Ann proffered. Heather was not the sort of person with whom one imposed deadlines but rather, like a wayward Jack Russell, needed to be coaxed into obedience.

"We'll go and get a coffee and talk it over. Then I'll call you, Ann. Thank you for your input. ... And you", she added less enthusiastically in the direction of Phoebe. "It is up to Graham now."

When they had gone the room suddenly felt reinvigorated, as if a window had been opened on the first warm spring day of the year after a particularly pernicious winter.

"I thought they'd be pleased" Phoebe said to Ann as she stood up, indignantly straight-backed. "Most people would jump at the chance of a donor organ."

"They might say yes."

Phoebe was not so sure. Oh well, that was up to them. It made no difference to her.

"Graham Eriksson's been very unlucky" Ann murmured, reaching for the computer mouse with which to pull up the list of other possible recipients on the screen, all of them deserving, all of them desperate.

"He has" agreed Phoebe wholeheartedly. "Heather Eriksson is appalling."

"I meant in getting BPC. The odds are against it – isn't it usually women who get it? Aren't 9 out 10 sufferers female?"

"Oh. I'd have to check the exact numbers but yes, I can accept that as an accurate ballpark ratio."

Just admit I'm right Ann thought as she studied the screen. One name stood out – Amber Kowalski.

"We'd better check who's next on the list who'll be a match. I just hope that they..." (Phoebe could not bring herself even to spit the Eriksson's name) "don't expect to be given any sort of donor priority if they refuse."

"Already on it" Ann said to the door as it closed behind the illustrious professor and she began googling universities in Queensland.

CHAPTER NINE

The canteen was noisy and metallic, from the chime of the cutlery to the tympani of the trays and the clumsy footwork of the furniture against the shiny floor. It was busy and relaxed, a place for people to sit down away from patients and beds, desks, computers, machinery and medicine. But not monitors. CCTV, like the rest of the hospital, was discreetly evident everywhere; modern cobwebs in corners and high places. But the food was good in a canteen sort of way: predictable, consistent, affordable, occasionally nutritious. When it was first opened, all stainless steel, hanging lights and battle ship grey paintwork, the epitome of Hospital Chic, tea and coffee had been only available from a self-service machine resulting in rebellion as close to mutiny as was legal in the NHS. Consequently, management had bowed (almost graciously) to pressure and tea and coffee could also be obtained from the canteen staff. These blue-clad, blue-hatted, latex-gloved beings could have come straight from an operating theatre but instead of bodies, they opened, doctored, sealed and closed the (mostly) edible.

You never quite knew who you might find there but Ann was not choosy. It was lunchtime (not that that featured much in the average twelve-hour shift) so chances were that there would be at least one person to whom she could impart her recent discoveries about la Dennington. Preferably someone with a propensity to gossip. Needless to say, Ann was not one of those; she dealt in facts. Although gossip was delicious - not that Phoebe did not deserve it but it would not be Ann who said as much. No, it was with a clear conscience that Ann entered the light, shiny bright room and surveyed its contents.

There was a – what would you call a collection of nurses, a divination, a charge? - making a great deal of noise in the middle but the tables around them were relatively quiet. Sitting at one of them, studying her mobile phone was Betsy Jones. Perfect! She and Ann were, if not good friends, certainly more than well acquainted. Occasionally they met up for a drink outside the hospital and had once gone to the cinema, or at least Ann had arranged it but Betsy had cried off at the last minute. Man trouble she had said. But then Fergus Crombie was always Trouble and although she was not supposed to know anything about his relationship with Betsy, it was obvious to anyone who knew her. She was a dead giveaway. So Ann had sat through the film on her own and found she enjoyed it more that way. She could lose herself in the screen without the pressure of another presence close to her. Too close. But she would say nothing about the Crombie-Jones liaison until she had solid facts at her disposal.

Waving her own mobile at the table she indicated to Betsy that she would get something to eat then join her. Would Betsy like something from the counter? No, thanks; Betsy put her hand firmly over her cup of coffee. Absolutely nothing for her. Ann's company might be unavoidable but no one was going to make her eat. It seemed to Ann, however, that Betsy was happy enough to see her and even slightly relieved. Or was she imagining things? Well, she would soon provide distraction and entertainment for even the most sombre of audiences and it was with a jaunty flat-footed step that she picked up one of the nearly clean trays and started her journey to the salad bar.

Happy New Year. And you. How was your Christmas? Clear the small talk and conventions out of the way then move in slowly, gently, innocuously and most of all, as if it meant nothing whatsoever. Ann began to chat about her morning; back to the coal face; they never really got away from it did they? Betsy agreed but it was all part of the job wasn't it? What they'd signed up for! But better not go there (shared laugh) although the Midland Central was a pretty good place to work and that made such a difference didn't it? Oh yes, absolutely Betsy agreed, thinking of Fergus. Out of interest though, had Betsy ever considered working abroad Ann wanted to know. She had toyed with the idea at the start of her career but had family commitments nearby so it had never really been an option. No, Betsy was the same she said and glanced at her mobile again.

"I'm expecting a call too" Ann said. Betsy said nothing. "About the donor liver we're expecting. You've worked with Phoebe Dennington quite a lot, haven't you?"

Yes, she had. Betsy looked at Ann with suspicion. Where was this going?

Ann was the picture of interested innocence. She had had no idea that Phoebe had worked in Australia! What an opportunity; must have been fascinating. No, she did not know exactly when or for how long but it must have been in Queensland because that was where she had got her professorship.

Stunned silence. Betsy stared.

"Coolangatta University".

"Are you sure?"

"She said so herself".

"God, is that the time? I must go." Betsy, suddenly proactive, standing up, chair pushed back, feet in motion, thumbs texting as she went. Ann smiled, stirred her tea and began to pick at her salad.

Phoebe avoided the canteen whenever possible. Sometimes, in the interests of team morale and hospital politics, one was obliged to visit and to look as if one was enjoying oneself. The tea was bad, the coffee worse and the so-called food that was churned out was of the lowest common denominator – mass appeal, cheap ingredients, bottled taste. At least it was consistent. Today however, the prospect of enforced *bonhomie* over the arrival of another New Year – Good God, it was an annual event; why all the fuss? – was more than Phoebe could bear so she went straight from Ann's office (so twee) to her own more ascetic, personal space. It was one of the few perks of her professorship – a room of one's own. Small, private, sacrosanct. Ann's office was not really hers but the province of the Recipient Co-ordinators whose sole unifying quality appeared to be their reprehensible taste in cutesy calendars supported by an endless quantity of boxes (not even tins) of assorted sweet biscuits. It would be nice to think that they were there for the benefit of their clients but one could never be sure.

She did not hear the door open behind her and Fergus come in. He ran his hand ever so lightly down her spine, from the base of her neck all the way to the small of her back, letting his fingers drift away as he reached her tailbone. A feather light touch, sensual, firm yet soft: his calling card.

"Fergus." Phoebe never even looked away from her computer screen and the music of the keyboard did not falter. "Happy New Year" she said to the words of the report she was writing. "How was your Christmas?" For a moment the screen was confused – to whom was she speaking? Computers did not celebrate Christmas as a rule; it was outside their programming. It must be the other person in the room that she meant. Even Fergus hesitated for a moment and wondered if he should repeat the caress along her back, perhaps from bottom to top? But no, that was Phoebe. Not outside the bedroom. Fergus felt like a school boy with a mediocre report card – tries hard but could do better.

"I'm waiting for a call.... Donor liver.... Could be interesting" Phoebe said to the perplexed computer.

Fergus wondered if he could tell her how he'd been on-call over the Christmas period as well as New Year because, like her, he did not have any family he wanted to speak of (or to), and how he had spent a most enjoyable and instructive (all too rare a combination) couple of nights with a student nurse, not to mention a variety of other less memorable sexual encounters over the festive period. Thank God for Tinder. He could regale her with accounts of bizarre patients in even more bizarre predicaments who had provided yet more beyond-belief material for research, medical initiative and canteen hilarity. Just when you thought you'd seen it all... But no. Not Phoebe.

"Interesting?"

"Yes. Chosen recipient is a possible no show. Well, his wife is."

"Sorry?"

There was a catch in Phoebe's answering silence and she thrashed the keyboard with increased pace. Meticulous documentation of the meeting with the Erikssons that had just finished was essential. Phoebe was not going to be held responsible for anything that might follow, not where the likes of Heather Eriksson were concerned. She only hoped that Ann Williams had enough sense to do the same. Fergus heard the message of the keys and threw in the towel.

"I'll leave you to it then. ... Just wanted to say hello.... I'll text."

"Yes. Why not?"

And he was dismissed.

"Why?" he was thinking as he crept out as unseen as he had arrived. "Is it because she makes it so bloody difficult?"

Outside in the corridor he stopped, bored, not sure where to go. Left towards the canteen or right to the staff room? Glancing right he espied the black legged FY1 with the generous chest and made as if to step in that direction. Except that she had seen him first and was even now swinging herself around pink-faced to return from whence she had come. He noticed that she was wearing a high-necked jumper: no buttons to buckle under the strain of containment. What a pity. It would serve her right if she ended up sweaty and uncomfortable after a shift in the hot-house temperatures on surgical. He wheeled left and headed for the canteen examining the texts on his phone before swiping into Tinder.

Ann was in conflict. To cake or not to cake? She had had a salad: healthy, nutritious, worthy. So far so good, but she would be hungry in an hour and unable to resist the biscuits in the office which would throw her calorie controlled not-diet (definitely not diet) but regimen. If she had a piece of cake now, a small piece (there was nothing larger in the canteen anyway) then she might last until her evening meal. She would never be as slim as the Betsys or Phoebes of this world; her collar bones would never be angular and hollow; her wrists would always be big and her feet like canoes. But she would not be fat either in her mind or anyone else's. (Except la Dennington). So she would have that piece of cake. Leaving her seat in such a way as made it very much occupied if anyone else should think of appropriating it, she headed back to the counter. No need for a tray – just a plate would be enough and would clearly indicate that she was merely adding to her meal, not starting out all over again. People were so quick to judge. Senior management and Public Health England (whatever that actually was) were obsessed with the weight of NHS personnel. Apparently, it was the tip of the social iceberg; the people had to be led by example so everyone in the NHS was to be perfectly formed. Body Mass Index had become the new social and professional denominator – you were either In or you were Over. Badges had been mooted for the Overs, currently being trialled in GP's surgeries. "I'm fat but working on it" they proclaimed. Might as well put them in orange jumpsuits

Before she had even picked up a plate her phone rang. It was Heather Eriksson. Perhaps she had seen Ann heading towards the carbs, or maybe she was telepathic. Wouldn't put anything past her. Whatever it was, the call had to be taken and the cake would have to wait.

CHAPTER TEN

"You're sure?"

"Yes."

"We have to act now. There's no room for delay."

"Yes darlin'. I know."

Betsy was talking to Ted. Her father had surprised her by phoning during the day. He knew she would be working, or sleeping before or after working, and was paranoid about 'disturbing her' or being a 'a bother', so hardly ever rang, but waited for her to contact him. If only he would learn to text...he had the wherewithal, Betsy had provided it but making and receiving calls on an iPhone was more than he could manage and even that had required intensive tuition. All of which he promptly forgot so returned to his ancient pay as you go which he understood and which had green and red nail varnish on the appropriate buttons so that he could ring out and then end the call.

"Have you told Lizzie?"

"No darlin', she's that busy and wouldn't know what to do."

Lizzie was the half-sister, also called a derivative of Elizabeth which annoyed the hell out of both of them. All they wanted to do was be as different from each other as possible.

"Look Dad, I'm about to go into theatre. I'll call as soon as I've finished. Stay calm."

"Don't you be worrying about me. I'm fine."

But she was worrying and he wasn't and they both knew. Not with that amount of blood which, it appeared, had been going on for some time. He'd thought it might be piles or something; didn't like to go to the doctor about down there and anyway, getting an appointment was impossible and how would he get there? No, of course he couldn't tell the warden. Nosy parker; it would be all round the place in no time and he couldn't stand the fuss. And what if it was a woman doctor? Yes, he knew that Betsy was a woman doctor but that was completely different and he hadn't said anything before because he knew she was so busy. She had her own life to lead.

Betsy had returned his call on her way to scrub up for theatre 4. The patient was scheduled for a Whipple's – a pancreaticoduodenectomy, depending on what they found when they opened her up. Whatever they discovered, the lady on the table would lose a substantial part of her digestive system and Betsy would be tied up keeping her alive for anything up to five hours depending on the complexity of a procedure that was never straight forward at the best of times and whether the surgeon knew what they were doing. It would require total and sustained concentration on her part. Her father would have to be put aside. Not forgotten but compartmentalised. Standard procedure for effective medics and clinicians and Betsy was good at it, except where Fergus was concerned.

"They've refused."

"I can't say I'm surprised. But they do realise they can't change their minds, the Erikssons? That this is final?"

Ann thought so but, and here she hesitated, perhaps it might be a good idea just to confirm with them that this was indeed their choice and that there was no going back? Professor Dennington was very anal about being given advice by minions but to her surprise, Phoebe agreed, apparently genuinely, and even indicated that she thought it was a sensible idea. Did Ann know where the Erikssons were? Phoebe would like to see them again, in her office this time, for a final discussion. A last chance saloon take it or leave offer as it were. As soon as possible. Now.

Ann would find them.

Meanwhile, who had Ann identified as a possible alternative? ... Amber Kowalski, 35, mother of two young children .... Right, Phoebe would take a look at the case.

They had all squeezed uncomfortably into Professor Dennington's *bijou* office; the nameplate beside the door was not much larger than the room itself. Phoebe sat behind her desk at her most professorial; Heather and Graham Eriksson were perched on hard chairs designed for speed rather than comfort while Ann stood sentry at one side, like a benevolent bouncer. Coffee and tea had not been offered; biscuits there were none.

Phoebe was courteous but formal, severe; seriously business like. How glad she was that she always wore executive suits. One never knew when such occasions would arise. She respected the Eriksson's decision – of course she did – she just wanted to be absolutely certain that they knew what they were doing and what the consequences might be. Did Phoebe realise that she was addressing Heather as she spoke? Ann wondered. Graham somehow seemed not to be there. Perhaps he wished he wasn't, especially when his wife replied.

"Are you questioning our judgement?"

No, of course not. They just wanted to be sure.

"We know perfectly well what we are doing, thank you Professor Dennington. Are you doubting our ability to make the right decision for us and our family? Because that's what it sounds like."

Again, no. More firmly said. The room felt very cold especially when silence descended like snow; even the air was muffled.

"No one doubts your ability, Mrs Eriksson" Ann interposed, attempting a thaw. Alas, a blizzard had set in.

"You offer us a sub-standard liver and are surprised when we refuse? What did you expect?" Heather's outrage swirled around the room, drifting into corners, piling up on Phoebe's desk, settling on the floor so that Graham moved his feet closer together and stared at them, as if to stop them freezing.

From behind her bulwark Phoebe retaliated with icy angular politeness.

"The demand for donor organs is very high. We just want to be sure that in refusing this one, you know that there is no guarantee that there will another."

'We' thought Ann, when did it become 'we'? She folded her arms against the chill.

"Of course there will be another" Heather retorted, "if we are prepared to wait. And we are. We're not unreasonable". If her final comment was offered as some sort of conciliatory gesture it failed; Phoebe had taken umbrage.

"But Graham might not be a priority at that point so it could be an extremely long wait, in which time his condition might seriously deteriorate."

"What do you mean, might not be a priority?" Heather was incredulous. She put her hand on her husband's shoulder as if to restrain him in the unlikely event of him leaping to his feet to object. Ann flung herself into the whirling snow, heroism that went completely unnoticed. She might as well have remained behind the ropes and let herself disappear into the churn. Nevertheless, she gave it a go.

Loss of priority was by no means a foregone conclusion Mrs Eriksson – Heather – she urged. It would have to be discussed. Phoebe glared at the Recipient Co-ordinator. 'Now you've done it' her face said.

"Discussed? What is there to discuss?" Heather turned on Ann.

Phoebe also stabbed Ann with an 'I told you so' look which was even colder than the air around them as Heather continued.

"Graham's a top priority and that's the way it stays. This liver isn't suitable so it goes to someone else and he's offered the next one."

"It's not quite as simple as that Mrs Eriksson". Phoebe now stepped back into the ring, spoke, and braced herself.

"Isn't it? Who says? You?"

"It's a joint decision made by all the organ donor agencies and personnel here, at the hospital, in the best interests of our patients. Somebody could become sicker and therefore gain a higher priority or we could add somebody new to the list who usurps your husband."

"What about the best interests of Graham?"

All eyes turned on the hapless victim, examining his cold feet as he twisted his thin yellow-tinted hands, squeezing his palms with his thumbs until both went white. Bony knuckles protruding from sparse flesh mapped with lumpy veins.

Phoebe, almost kindly, wanted to know what he thought about it. Then, to Ann's surprise, how he felt about it. He continued to writhe through his hands for a moment before he spoke, addressing his feet. His wife's hand still rested on his shoulder.

"The same as Heather" he said eventually, not looking up. Her hand moved very slightly as if to pat him, rewarding good behaviour. He continued, this time addressing Phoebe. "Not just because she's my wife but because I have the right to choose according to what is best for me and my family."

There, told you! Heather was triumphant and the snow swirled afresh. She released her grip on Graham and the strings slackened; he slumped forward as if trying to get closer to the comfort of his shoes. Heather however, straightened even more and surveyed the field. Like all good commanders she had courage and insight – seize the moment, capitalise on success, smash them to pieces. She focussed on the leader of the opposition – take them down from the top.

"And you have no right to penalise him for making a decision you don't like. It goes against the Patient's Charter. I trained as a nurse so I know. Patients have the right to autonomy over medical decisions. It's Graham's body. Not yours."

Or yours Ann thought but kept quiet; she would be a loyal second to her leader in this one-to-one but it was up to Phoebe now. The meeting had taken an ugly downward turn and it was up to the Professor to deal with it: the privilege of rank. Who'd be a professor now? Phoebe apparently; nothing she liked better. And she had form. Tilting her head ever so slightly to one side she looked at Heather as if curious and replied, almost conversationally,

"You must have trained before 2000 then, when the NHS Constitution for England replaced the Patient's Charter."

Everything froze, whether from fear or the icy temperature in the room was impossible to say. Graham's hands were a tableau of yellow and white knuckled distress, suspended at the end of his arms like badly-mixed ice-cream. Ann's eyebrows had risen to her hairline as if reaching for protective cover. She stared with enthralled horror first at Phoebe then at Heather. Graham's eyes had closed against Armageddon and, Phoebe? Phoebe just continued to half smile at her opponent.

The cloud burst.

"How dare you patronise me! My husband is a priority and that doesn't change, not for any reason. He has the right to be the first choice for any donor liver and I want it confirmed, in writing, otherwise we will be forced to take action. No one dictates to me or my family. Come on Graham; we're leaving.... This does not end here."

The blizzard made its way out of the door but the temperature in the room descended even further.

CHAPTER ELEVEN

Theatre 4 was ready and waiting; the patient prepped and prone like a prop waiting in the wings to be brought out onto the stage at the appropriate moment for the drama to proceed: a handkerchief to be dropped, a handbag to be found – the one thing without which the performance cannot function, including the actors. Betsy and her assistant were at the head of the table, their place setting being inspected, prepared and checked. The supporting cast led by the theatre sister were already assembled in readiness for the arrival of the lead surgeon and his first assistant who led the way into the room, gloved hands aloft like a Croc-soled John the Baptist announcing the arrival of the Messiah. I am just the herald he seemed to say, behind me comes He Who Matters, the Saviour. Jeremy Albright. Otherwise known as JA (in his hearing) and Jack Ass everywhere else

Betsy had worked with (or rather, for) JA several times and had become used to his *modus operandi*. All surgeons had them, it went with the territory, like handwriting. Same words, different style – some neat and precise, others more florid with curly loops and bold detached capital letters or all joined up with hardly any gaps. Some of the most experienced had developed a form of shorthand which produced the same text but in less time, like a form of speed writing. In the end it actually made little difference to the surgical outcome but did affect the way the lead surgeon interacted with his team, who knew him, his style and what to expect. JA certainly had a style that was very much his own (no one else wanted it) which focussed not so much on his surgical techniques but more on his person. He was, as one colleague had put it, the final victory of style over substance. Not that he was incompetent; Betsy was the first to acknowledge his skill and reliability at the operating table. A solid, dependable jobbing surgeon; salt of the hospital earth, conscientious and careful; extremely well qualified as everyone was made to know. He was married to the redoubtable Vikki, a nurse, who worked part-time in Imaging which, as the more sceptical among them agreed, was preternaturally appropriate. If anything, Vikki cared more about her husband's image than JA himself. Certainly, she never stopped talking about it which, expressed in her undeniably Midlands accent, caused a great deal of speculation about the nature of their union. They did not have children so she couldn't even have been pregnant when they got married.

JA made his way onto the stage and took his place at the centre of the table. He had met the patient for the first time that morning in pre-prep and had been able to reassure her about the procedure to come. Yes, it was a bit tricky but nothing he had not done before and he had every confidence in a successful outcome. He also had two very competent registrars to assist. She had seemed nervous but not unintelligent so he had told her about his PhD from Oxford and that had calmed her. She was not his patient as such but, yes, he had carefully studied her case and she need have no concerns. Of course the mass – a tumour he clarified for her benefit - attached to her pancreas would be removed – he would see to it himself. What? She had been told that they wouldn't know exactly what was going on until they opened her up? Well! He didn't know who had told her that but she needn't have any concerns – none at all. He had looked at her notes and her case, knew what to expect, what to do and how to do it. There. So, no need to worry! He would see her just before she went into theatre, before the anaesthetist got to work, and then again when it was all over. Now she was unconscious and nothing more than an uneven green sheeted shape before him, the site of the incision and procedure the only part of her flesh to be seen. A job to be done.

JA opened proceedings as he made an incision into the abdomen. A slightly curved, deft slice, about 20 cm long, wielding the scalpel like a pen, confident and assured: his trademark. It was a sacred moment to which he often referred when he had an audience. That moment when he, and he alone, could enter a hidden private world unseen by anyone else. It was a privilege accorded only to a very few. No number of scans or X Rays could compete in terms of knowledge and revelation. Surgeons were the fast jet pilots of the medical profession, which was why only the very best made it to the top which was not only a place of privilege but also of great responsibility. He liked to talk as he worked, to share his thoughts; it was instructive for his surgical assistants and the team in general, as well as anyone who might be observing from the rear. He encouraged observation – always best to learn by example he told his students, especially by the best. They might even find themselves in the same position as himself one day, if they worked hard and applied themselves, and you never knew when learning by osmosis would make the difference between success and failure.

Betsy had heard most of it before, as had the team with whom JA regularly worked. Sometimes there were problems putting together enough people to be in theatre with him but those who were there today were mostly seasoned hands who had long since developed the facility to function effectively, apparently attentively, while thinking their own thoughts to the impairment of everything that came out of JA's mouth. Only the assistant surgeons had to be seen to be listening. At least we're all wearing masks Betsy thought and smiled to herself. Each reg was competent, clearly there to assist rather than be trained and she had every expectation that she would be out of theatre in a few hours at most. Then she could call her father and deal with the real issue of the day. But not now. Concentrate she chastised herself sternly, promptly put Ted in a mental box and shut the lid.

"So now I'm beginning the Kocherisation of the duodenum" JA narrated as he rummaged inside the incision, the fingers of one hand probing and pulling between the retractors holding open the red, pink and yellow fat-lined orifice. The sight of an open incision always reminded Betsy of Geography lessons– those cross-section diagrams of multi-coloured strata, cut in half to reveal layers of colour encasing the secretive base structure. JA might have been telling an oft read bedtime story he was so relaxed and comfortable with his script. Absolute confidence he would tell everyone – that's the secret. If I'm confident with what I'm doing then everyone else will be too: leadership comes from the top. He continued his narrative for the benefit of his audience. Sadly, the only person in the room who did not understand Kocherisation was the patient and she was unlikely to remember what he had said.

"That means I'm dissecting the duodenum so that I can locate and remove the mass adhering to the head of the pancreas. Both will be removed together." He could have been a small boy looking for a lost screw in a half-built Meccano construction as he wiggled and twisted his hands under the metal retractors straining like cranes over the edges of the hole.

"Ah! Inevitably, the real thing never looks quite like the textbook" he joshed as he lifted the pancreas. It moved, free and light, blinking slightly in the unexpected light and freedom; unencumbered and alone apart from its attached friend the duodenum. The mass that they were looking for remained behind, stolid and fixed. You'll have to do better than that it seemed to mock as it stuck firmly to the IVC - Inferior Vena Cava - the main vein returning blood to the heart from the lower half of the body.

Silence. Not even music in the background – JA preferred quiet in theatre. Music distracted; he liked to be heard. Some surgeons claimed that music reduced stress and helped focus the mind, especially during lengthy procedures but JA felt it was a gimmick; real surgeons did not listen to music. The mass, about the size of a grapefruit, stared defiantly up at the surgeon and clung onto the vein pulsating from its nearby colleague, the aorta with whom it had grown up and to which it had become very attached. Where I go, he goes too it said to the surgeon. We're in this together. It had taken the best part of an hour for JA to mobilise the head of the pancreas and to determine the upper and lower borders of the belligerent mass only to discover now that it was fixed to the IVC at precisely the same point as the right renal vein so it was not only the IVC that would have to be reconstructed, the whole of the right kidney would have to come out too.

JA did not swear. It was a point of principle for him never to use bad language. A man with a PhD could always find a more civilised alternative to the common parlance of anger, frustration and vulgarity but on this occasion even he was taken aback. So he remained silent and stared at the recalcitrant tumour while his team looked first at the contents of the hole, then at their leader and finally at each other. This was a most unexpected turn of events and, to the regs' delight, quite exciting. This would be one to discuss in the canteen and the pub, particularly as everything depended on JA and how he dealt with it. To remove the mass meant removing a section of the IVC and the right kidney which had sworn allegiance to the enemy and joined forces with it, taking its blood supply with it like a medieval lord at the head of his army of tenant farmers. It would be a bloody conflict to the death if mishandled and as JA had said himself, the real thing never looked quite like the textbook diagrams. What the hell was what? The regs were damned if they knew. They turned their gaze to JA: over to you, boss.

The first thing to do was find and tie off the right renal artery

- scary stuff for someone not used to doing it. Then clamp off the IVC above the mass but below the origin of the left renal vein and above the top edge of the tumour. And not only that but also clamp the IVC below the mass. Both of these required the vena cava to be dissected from its friendly tethering, avoiding those pesky little veins that you couldn't see draining blood from the spine. No road map, no directions, no textbook diagrams and everything to play for. One false move and it might all be over; game set and match. Only then could the process of dividing and removing the inseparable companions *en-bloc* be carried out. But that was then.

"Press!" JA told the reg opposite him across the table; "we need continuous pressure to control the blood flow. ... You're not doing it properly ... Press!"

JA in turn pressed his gaze on the point where the right renal artery was attached to the aorta. Nothing moved except the blood heaving against the clamp. The reg was incompetent! The other one no better. Thankfully no one could see the riot going on in JA's head where full-scale war had broken out. Even though in possession of hugely superior numbers, Confidence had been assaulted by Fear, backed up by Failure and Humiliation which were rapidly acquiring recruits in the form of Inexperience and Panic. JA urgently needed reinforcements. In his defence however, Decision could at least still act and he had an armoury of Bravado to back it up.

"This is a most interesting turn of events" he heard himself saying, as if watching the drama from front row stalls. "Obviously we'll have to proceed in a completely different direction... Fascinating... In fact, before we continue, I think I'll ask Professor Dennington to attend. She'll be keen to observe a procedure involving the IVC as part of her ongoing liver transplant training ... Keep the pressure steady and continuous" he said to the heavily sweating reg who was manning the clamps like an all-in wrestler. "Stabilise the patient" he casually instructed Betsy, "while I step out and give Professor Dennington a call". He addressed the room, as if the walls would step in to replace him. Then he was gone.

JA was on the phone almost as soon as he left theatre.

"Perhaps you could pop down and help? The assistant isn't up to the task; it's impossible for me to see what's happening ... just a little light bleeding ... it'd certainly be an interesting case for you."

He was outlining the events of theatre 4 and Phoebe was listening, occasionally interrupting, with increasing irritation. She really was extremely busy. The Erikssons had finally left the premises but left behind more paperwork than any one family had ever deserved. She was a liver transplant surgeon not Red Adair, but JA was a colleague, a senior member of staff and tipped to be their next Medical Director so she really ought to take his request seriously. He also had a PhD, from Oxford no less, which rather clinched the matter. Besides, she might be able to put her name to a research paper out of it so yes, she would be delighted to attend. A quick call to her Recipient Co-Ordinator and then she would be there immediately.

Like the others, Betsy had been astonished by JA's sudden disappearance. Even though she, as the senior anaesthetist could actually overrule him and stop any surgical procedure on medical grounds if the patient developed breathing problems, this rarely happened and for the lead surgeon to abandon his post at such a critical point, leaving his assistant to hold back the tide was almost unprecedented. At least this patient was stable and the reg, although sweaty, panting and somewhat dishevelled, was maintaining the pressure. He did not look happy, even behind his mask which was billowing in and out over his mouth and nose until he looked as if he might swallow himself with it, so deep were his inhalations. Clearly this was not going to be a quick fix; they were going to be here for hours and after care was going to take longer than originally anticipated. The arterial line which had been inserted into the patient for close monitoring was clearly going to be insufficient so Betsy would have to insert a central line into the woman's neck, straight into the jugular. If she could find it. All she could see was a tangle of green sheets.

It was not that she couldn't do it, she just wanted to be sure that she could and that she did and that she did it properly. The departure of their captain when it looked as if the boat might sink had done little to boost team confidence and morale. Betsy beckoned to her ODP – operating department practitioner – a lovely man but newly qualified. Keen, energetic, willing but not yet terribly able. What she needed was experience so she very quietly asked him to call down for someone to assist. He leapt to the task; the thought of putting in a central line had brought him out in almost as much sweat as the reg with the clamp.

Just as it reached the point where it was obvious that something was going to give – either the reg or the clamp, it was hard to choose - but the aorta was definitely going to win, JA returned to post. Serene, confident, self-assured he exuded genial *gravitas* as he announced that they would shortly be joined by Professor Dennington so would wait for her to arrive before proceeding. Fortunately she arrived almost immediately, scrubbed, gloved, irked and ready for action. One glance at the *tableau* around the table and she knew exactly why she had been so eagerly summoned. The reg entwined with the clamp and pressing on the aorta was in a near state of collapse. The aorta, sensing victory, had redoubled is efforts in the face of the enemy and was throbbing with enthusiasm. 'A little light bleeding!' Under her mask Phoebe scowled at JA; eyes narrowed to knife blades she went straight to where he stood and elbowed him aside.

"For a better view" she hissed and took his place. The reg opposite gazed at her with adoration and dared to hope. Likewise all the others circled around the near-calamity. Even the table seemed sturdier, more resolute, less likely to fold under the stress. Only JA seemed not to notice. He stood back, a little, so that Phoebe had to shove him away from her as she began her errand of mercy by tying off veins and arteries.

"Elbows!" she barked at him and he removed the offending appendages with the rest of their companions to a more distant point behind from whence he could observe and continue to comment.

"You talk and I'll do the actions" Phoebe muttered.

If those of the team near her heard, they gave no sign but, in the canteen, corridors, nurses' stations and staff room later it became something of a catchphrase.

"Central line?" Phoebe tilted her head vaguely in the direction of Betsy as she rummaged thoughtfully inside the gore that identified as an abdomen. Betsy nodded and also began to rummage, not inside but outside the upper part of the body swathed in the amorphous green sheets.

"Let me."

Betsy froze. It was Fergus. Beside her, leaning over, so close she could feel his pulse, the warmth of his skin, hear and touch and taste the scent of his body as it sang to her.

"Your ODP called" he whispered as he stood as close to her as the scrubs she was wearing. "I knew it was you so I came..."

Was he being lewd? It was impossible to tell but her body tingled even as he located the flesh they needed. Exposing a smooth patch of sinewy neck on the patient he placed his index finger on the site of the jugular and pressed very slightly so that the flesh became pale under his touch.

"Here" he said. "I'll let you push it in."

She shivered inside her thin clothes and pressed her thighs together to maintain control. With tensed knees and raised toes from heels cemented to the sterile floor she girded her resolve and began the process of inserting a tube into the pulsating blood flow. Fergus held the patient's skin firm, taut, tight as she eased in first the needle then the tube to which she attached the portals which then hung, fuchsia like, surrounded by fabric greenery. Only then did Fergus move away, leaving her as moist and flustered as the reg with the clamp.

He of the aforementioned almost embraced the lofty Professor when Phoebe announced that the aorta (by now extremely disgruntled) was under control and that he could stand down, as it were, for a breather and let his colleague take over by applying clamps above and below the mass so that she could remove it. JA was not even consulted, never mind invited to assist. He continued to narrate, like a Greek Chorus as she proceeded to divide and rule, incise and remove – tumour, kidney, IVC and all. The temptation to slap the erudite owner of the PhD from Oxford into submission then sever him from the room was almost unbearable so Phoebe was relieved that she had to concentrate very hard on the task in hand. The tumour was reluctant to move – quite comfortable where he was, thank you, happy to stay - you'll have to pick me out bit by bit if you want me to go. Which is what she did.

If she had noticed that Fergus was in the room, she gave no hint of recognition. Even he was not sure if she had seen him but knew better than to interrupt as she was operating. One of the things he admired about her – found irresistible – was her absolute professionalism – clinical, meticulous and self-absorbing. She needed no one, especially not him and it drove him to distraction. It was the ultimate aphrodisiac. At that moment he wanted nothing else than to be with her, hand in hand, foraging inside a stranger.

JA was waxing lyrical as he gave a running commentary on Phoebe's every action. Safe in the wings, dressed for the part but out of danger he was the perfect principal understudy: word perfect, on cue, projecting his voice to every corner of the auditorium so that he could easily be heard. He gave an expert delivery – not too fast, variety of tone for interest with clear diction and pauses at all the appropriate moments. Phoebe was the film and he the subtitles, and she wanted to kill him.

"So now Professor Dennington is going to reconstruct the IVC. She has made a full circumferential excision and will use the blood group matched section of IVC that we have obtained from the transplant stock kept in cold storage on site. So important for unforeseen situations such as this."

The eyebrows of the surgical team danced over the top of their masks. He means the fridge in theatre 3 they said to each other and pretended not to laugh. But JA did not notice. He was too busy talking.

"It's important – and I know the Professor will agree with me" (no one dared look at her) "to trim the replacement section to size but always a little shorter than it at first appears as it stretches when filled with blood. That's a detail ..." (this directed to the two regs.) "that comes with experience." Phoebe looked as if she would have liked to trim him to well below size then fill him with anything that would make him stretch, preferably to the point of eruption. "Now she's tying off any tributaries" (dramatic pause) ... "and will perform a leak test with saline.... There, see how it stretches?" They watched, they saw, their eyebrows soared as he continued: "Professor Dennington is doing an excellent job. Textbook. Notice how she is repairing any holes before she sutures the two ends together with 4/0 prolene, starting at the middle of the back wall."

At this point Phoebe could bear no more. She indicated to the assisting reg that he should ease off the superior clamp and check for bleeding. If it was okay, he could remove the other clamp, surround the connections with arterial mops, wait a few minutes and the show was all but over. When JA shouted "Bingo" as the procedure was completed her face darkened, she gripped her gloved hands together so as not to tighten them around JA's throat and swallowed hard, possibly as an attempt to prevent herself from saying something regrettable. Fergus watched her entranced. Betsy watched Fergus, equally entranced and squeezed her thighs together ever harder.

CHAPTER TWELVE

Phoebe was the first to leave the theatre and thanked God that she did not have to share a changing room – any kind of room - with JA. At least she could strip and cleanse herself away from the odious man and if others heard her muttering as she transformed from creased blue, blood-spattered sawbones to sharp-suited expensively kitten-heeled professor well, they were welcome. Repeat what you like she said into her locker, possibly out of hearing, and left, texting Ann Williams as she went.

JA was gracious in his thanks to his team. It was always important to show appreciation; one of the first rules of successful management and central to his ethos of success. It had been a tricky procedure as well as much longer than anticipated and no doubt they were tired. But they should feel pleased with themselves; they had pulled (the reg with the clamp grimaced at the memory) together and he had no doubt that Professor Dennington had been impressed. On hearing this as she prepared the patient for transfer to ICU Betsy stopped, mid-manoeuvre and gaped. No other word for it. Was the man insane? Even Fergus who had stayed until Phoebe finished and then stayed even more, very close to Betsy which severely hampered her efficiency, was uncharacteristically taken aback. Then he found it amusing and had to leave the room to avoid embarrassing himself. To laugh at a time when the rest of the team were so mortified would have been insensitive, even by his standards. Had Phoebe known he was there? Still he was not sure but it was imperative to find out. Betsy would discuss the subject endlessly, in and out of bed which might initially be entertaining but it was Phoebe's take on events that he really wanted to hear. If he could get her to talk about it. There was no need to mention it to anyone else. The witnesses and especially the registrars would see to that. His only regret was that Senior Management might not get wind of it.

Phoebe however had other ideas. Ann Williams had called her and they had discussed the case of Amber Kowalski. It was an interesting one, not least because of the marginal nature of the donor organ. In addition to her current liver problems Amber had a history of cancer. Although now cancer free, her stage 2 melanoma had been successfully treated only 3 years before. Clinical wisdom designated a gap of 5 years between any form of cancer and a transplant in order to reduce the risk of rejection, immunosuppression and recurrence of cancer. On the other hand, Amber was stable, suitable and had a good chance of survival. She was also the mother of two young children, one of whom had not even started school and there was a teenager in the family, a boy of thirteen to whom Amber was stepmother. She was almost certain to welcome the opportunity for a transplant even with an organ rejected as inferior by the Erikssons. But what about her husband/partner/other half? Was there any such a person of whatever description currently residing in the household? Indeed there was Ann informed Phoebe, choosing to ignore the very non-pc implications of the enquiry. There was no Mr Kowalski but a partner called Agwe Dacosta, the father of the teenage boy. The good news was that there were no special problems with any of the children, especially the teenager; Ann had asked. Amber felt that the thirteen-year-old spent too much time on the internet and too little on his schoolwork but he was a great kid and a real help with the little ones.

"However..." Ann began.

A pause. The spectre of Heather Eriksson wafted into their joint consciousness and seemed to fill the room.

"Mr Dacosta..."

Phoebe feared the worst.

"He's Rasta."

Heather Eriksson was laughing at her, Phoebe could hear.

"But Rastafarians don't believe in organ donation and transplantation. It's against their religion...Why is she on the list?"

"I don't think Amber's Rasta, just her partner. But that's not the point, is it?"

Ann had no choice but to meet Phoebe head on. "She's on the list so we have to respect that..." Would she have to spell it out? God, she hoped not. Phoebe could be so ... annihilating. But they could not pick and choose a recipient on the list according to their religion.

"We'd better call them both in" Phoebe decided. "It's been hard to persuade the transplant team about Amber as a recipient so we need to know how she – and her partner – feel, especially as it's a marginal organ." The image of Heather grew larger and more defined; Phoebe's office felt crowded and cold.

"I'll get onto it now" Ann said with relief and escaped, leaving Phoebe to try and exorcise her work space.

Fergus and Betsy had gone in different directions once they left theatre 4. Fergus had left first – no sign of Betsy which was a relief as he had emerged from the male changing room. It had amused him to witness her discomfort and discombobulation when he had appeared at her side. Even below her mask, hat and gown her orgasmic flush had been obvious and he wondered who else might have noticed. Probably no one – JA and Phoebe were playing centre stage so none of the team would have been looking at the anaesthetists. Theatre staff never seemed to notice them at the best of times and certainly never when warring surgeons were the main attraction. The changing room had been unnaturally quiet whilst JA was there but as soon as he left, fashionably early as befitted the most important guest at a party, those that remained could relax and start to enjoy themselves. And they did. So much to say! Who would have believed it? The regs led the way, especially he of the clamp who was exhausted – utterly worn out – his arms ached – he had no idea how he'd kept going. People might criticise la Dennington but you had to hand it to her, she was good in a crisis whereas JA… He would say no more. He did not need to; everyone said it for him.

Fergus wondered how he could get a sneak preview of JA's written report of the event, for that is what it had become. The surgical procedure in itself was unusual and interesting but its medical significance paled in comparison to JA's stellar performance. He had outclassed even himself. What would the lovely Vikki think when she heard about it? For she surely would. It would be impossible not to. Imaging by its very nature and location was gossip central – everyone went there, it was full of cubby holes and dark corners, perfect for the furtive, the salacious and the scandalous. Which gave him an idea.

Betsy meanwhile had 'stepped out' for a moment herself. Completely. She was standing in the hospital grounds within sight and sound of the huge main entrance but far enough away to make it clear that she did not want to be disturbed. It was cold and dark; the days were short enough without the added complication of a prolonged surgical procedure to rob them of frail warmth and light. They had been in theatre for hours – almost seven in the end but longer for Betsy who had followed the patient from there into ICU to ensure that she could wake up, even for a moment. She was now 'sleeping' in a drug induced fog in the care of other hands so, finally, Betsy was able to make that call to Ted. Consumed by the guilt of neglect which wore her like skin, she was ashamed of her impatience when he did not immediately pick up.

"Dad! It's me."

"Hello Me".

"How are you?"

"Fine, lass. Just the same."

That was the problem. Betsy grimaced but kept it out of her voice.

"You need to see your GP, Dad. Have you made an appointment?"

No, he hadn't. Couldn't she do that? Yes, she could but it would have been better if he'd already done it, or Lizzie. Lizzie could have done it for him. Never mind, she would ring and get him in as soon as possible. She'd do it now - glancing at her watch. Just enough time to catch them if she was quick. Then she'd ring him back.

"But it's urgent. He must see a doctor."

"Is it an emergency? If it is, he needs to go to hospital."

Betsy wanted to scream at the receptionist, to howl and rail and throw thunderbolts at her. She hoped she kept fury out of her voice though; it hurt when patients spoke like that.

"He's passing large amounts of blood and needs to see a doctor who will almost certainly suspect cancer of the colon and make an emergency referral."

She heard the sneer at the other end of the phone.

"How do you know? Are you a doctor?"

"Yes" she said.

A silence followed. Betsy waited. The receptionist was deciding whether or not to believe her and, in the end, for the sake of an easy life and to avoid any kind of legal transgression, made a complete surrender and offered an appointment for the following morning.

"It's an urgent slot" she said, as graciously as bile permitted, "so if he doesn't need it please let us know so someone else can have it. We have lots of people who want to be urgent."

There was so much that she could have said but what was the point? Betsy had got what she wanted and called her father with the news. How would he get there he wanted to know? Lizzie could take him ... couldn't she? More silence. Betsy would arrange and pay for a taxi then. Another pause – the Jones' main means of communication which was so much more eloquent than words.

"So, I'll be on me own then, will I?"

"I'm sorry Dad. I can't get back just for that but I'll call as soon as you've seen him." Or her, Betsy kept to herself. They both knew Lizzie would be too busy and that neither of them dared to ask. "I've got to go, Dad. We'll speak tomorrow." And she left him – where? In the bathroom? In bed? Eating by himself at the kitchen table? He refused to have meals in front of the TV – said it was the last vestige of civilisation and her step-mother would have hated it. You know what she was like. Wouldn't even drink tea out of a mug. He kept her bone china cup and saucer on the table with the salt and pepper, even after all this time, so that he wouldn't have to eat alone.

Unlike Phoebe, who rather enjoyed a solitary repast, especially after the kind of day she had had. It gave her an opportunity to nurse her anger and rehearse what she would say to Hugh Goldberg when she complained about JA. Who thoroughly deserved his nick name and frankly, was lucky it was no worse. The Medical Director's secretary had left a message for her to make an appointment with him at her earliest convenience which had been a surprise, but not unpleasant. Senior managers were so pressed for time that more often than not it was necessary to arrange even routine meetings. Such were the rigours of responsibility in such an illustrious hospital. It was also opportune;

she needed to discuss the Erikssons insistence on retaining top recipient priority with Hugh. And now she felt professionally compelled to talk to him about JA who had been extremely fortunate (not to mention the patient) that she had been able to step in – literally – at such short notice. The appointment had been fixed for the day after next. Hugh must indeed be keen to see her. It was in his diary his secretary - surprisingly well spoken for a typist - had confirmed and the Medical Director was certain to seeing her.

All of which was very gratifying and as it should be. What would she wear? She had a new pencil skirt and matching tailored waist length jacket which had not yet made its hospital debut. That with the cream silk shirt and her trademark kitten heels would be perfect. Jewellery? Discreet – just earrings – the large pearls. Expensive, tasteful and discerning. Her mobile was on silent but shivered and bounced on the granite counter top of her kitchen – also expensive, tasteful and discerning – and she noted that it was Fergus. Three missed calls no less. Too bad. He would have to wait. She went upstairs to shower.

Initially, Betsy ate nothing but drank tea – out of a mug. She had hated her step mother who had not only usurped her own mother in her father's affection and his life but had brought Lizzie into the world. Both mothers were now dead but not forgotten, well, by her at least. And now she faced the prospect of losing her father. It could not happen; she could not let it happen. Even if she had to see Lizzie and they had to work together to save him.

She went to the fridge-freezer, opened the doors and pinned the lower one back with her foot while she gazed at the contents. Resolve got the better of her so she removed her foot and the doors swung back into place with relief as she picked up her phone and called Fergus' landline. No reply. Straight to answerphone. As always. Why the hell didn't he ever pick up? He could see it was her – the number would flash lurid red with the vigour of a sign giving directions to a brothel. He knew her number;

he'd called it often enough. She called his mobile. Unavailable. Please try later.

Betsy swore like a North Shields docker on the piss. Ted would have been proud of her. She hammered out a text message and punched the send button so hard that the phone tried to pitch itself out of her hand and jump to its death. Where was Fergus when she needed him? Betsy wept as she headed back to the fridge and flung the door aside, wedged it open with a chair and started to empty the contents, mostly onto the floor where she sat down and started to eat. Everything. Then she started on the freezer before moving on to the store cupboard. Two hours later, bloated, nauseous, humiliated and ashamed she took her distended stomach and food-stained body upstairs to the bathroom where she leant over the toilet bowl and stuck three fingers down her throat.

CHAPTER THIRTEEN

Phoebe was perplexed. But she was a professional and the hospital had a strict policy about the sanctity of religious beliefs for patients and staff alike. Amber Kowalski was on the list, she had priority and was in the unenviable position of making even a marginal organ a very attractive proposition. Although small framed, her ascites had made her more of a physical match for large man Alan's liver. As she had shuffled into the office Phoebe could see that her stomach was distended and protruded noticeably from her slender frame which seemed cowed by the weight of the fluid within. She had leant back as she stood, hands on wide waist as if heavily pregnant then dropped into a proffered chair with obvious relief. But what worried Phoebe more was the knowledge that they were running out of time for the transplant – the cold ischaemic time was jogging steadily to ground zero with the relentless determination of a seasoned long-distance runner and if it arrived before they did, there would be no liver for Amber or anyone else.

Even with her huge belly, Amber was as short and brittle as her partner was tall and slim, as pale and flaxen white as he was dark. Agwe wore his unrestrained dreadlocks and beard like a mane, leonine and ferocious as he loomed behind the chair over his partner and the mother of his children, but there the danger ended. His eyes were soft, his face smooth with geniality and his manners old school. Ann was enchanted, not least because at last she had found someone of equal height to whom she could converse at the same altitude. His hair was amazing – how did you get the hair to grow like that? How long had it taken? Agwe needed no further bidding and immediately launched into an extremely enthusiastic and lengthy account of the history, significance and upkeep of Rastafarian dreadlocks. They were sacred he said; it was in the Bible. Did she know the story of Samson? Yes, she did indeed but she'd had no idea that it was of such importance. So they believed that their strength lay in their hair? Did that mean they could not be washed? Agwe roared with a deep throated laugh and shook his mane. Man!

"We wash them at least twice a week – it's good for them. Shampoo gets rid of the oils and makes them tighter."

At this point, fascinating as it was, Phoebe acknowledged, she had no choice but to interrupt their chat and bring the meeting back to reality. Time really was of the essence. The marginal nature and condition of the donor liver had been fully, painstakingly explained to them with all the possible complications and consequences and now it was up to them to decide whether or not to accept it.

"Not me. Amber." Agwe said. "It's her body and her decision. She knows I'm happy with whatever she wants."

"Even though it's against Rastafarianism?" Ann asked.

"It's up to Amber. We're partners. Equals. She makes her own choices."

Phoebe smiled with impending relief and the hanging shadow of Heather Eriksson made as if ready to depart. Ann opened a celebratory box of biscuits and offered them to the guests, as if the sugar content would help influence a positive outcome but they proved to be unnecessary. While the potential recipient and her partner both declined a biscuit thank you – too much sugar and over processed for their organic tastes, Amber delivered the verdict. They had discussed it many times and again when Ann had called. It had been her choice to go on the transplant list in the first place and she was not going to change her mind now. Her cancer diagnosis three years before had brought home to her how much she valued life, how precious it was and now she would do anything to preserve it. Their children were young and needed her; Agwe needed her and she needed him. No, they would not be returning to Jamaica – the Midlands was their home now. She had family in the area and it had been exposure to the West Indian sun which had almost certainly caused her melanoma. The children were quite fair skinned so they had decided to make their home in Birmingham where there was less sun (hearty agreement all round) they could properly home school the kids and, crucially, she had access to the health care she needed. That she could not live without. And while she was managing, more or less, her cholangitis at the moment she knew that without a new liver it would only get worse. She looked ruefully at the stomach resting on her lap: at least it sometimes took her mind off the constant itching that tormented her waking life.

"It would be wrong to refuse" Amber explained. "Not when someone has given me such an opportunity ... and it might be my only chance, mighten it?"

No one disagreed. Especially not Agwe. He thanked Jah that it was not his decision to make, unsure how he would have chosen. Love of God and religion was a great way to live your life but that was it wasn't it? Having a life. Being alive. Something he had always taken for granted until he had met Amber and she had become ill in Jamaica, where she was only living to be with him. So they had moved to Birmingham where she had been treated and now here they were again, in hospital, which went against everything in which he believed but he did not want to lose her. He even wondered if – assuming the transplant worked and she recovered – whether he would be able to reconcile his conscience with opting out of organ donation as the new law would require. But in the end Jah would – and did – provide, so he'd go with it and support his wife all the way. Anyway, there was no point in overthinking the issue.

"Yeah" he said.

The first thing they had to do was get Amber admitted and run blood tests to establish suitability and match. Then, all being well (as anticipated), they could schedule her for surgery later that day. Yes, it had to be as soon as possible because of the cold ischaemic time – the organ could not wait. However, there was just one more thing that had to be considered. Amber did realise that she would have to take drugs – conventional medicine - for ever afterwards to prevent rejection and problems after the transplant? Phoebe appreciated that this might not conform to Rastafarian er, medical beliefs, but it was absolutely unavoidable. Amber would have to take painkillers and antibiotics after the surgery as well as a cocktail of oral drugs including steroids for the rest of her life; long term success depended upon it.

Yes, that was fine. She and Agwe agreed. A small price to pay. Could she see the children before she went into theatre?

"You said no?"

It was not quite the reaction Heather had expected from her daughter.

"It was your father's decision."

"Yeah, right."

Even Archie noticed the sudden collapse of his family. Graham mouthed 'Siobhan' in silent wonder, too shocked to give it voice. Then he turned a fearful gaze on his wife to see how she would react. Never in the history of the Eriksson's family life had a child spoken to a parent thus. Well, not that he knew and had certainly never witnessed. Archie too watched his mother as much out of curiosity as anything. Siobhan's contempt was palpable; she was also furious. But no match for her mother's answering fury. To be questioned in this way by a child was insupportable and she would not, absolutely would not, stand for it. The anticipated 'how dare you speak to me like that?' response began, initially quietly, then more sorrowfully as it progressed into the 'I'm so disappointed in you' phase that was usually enough to strangle any insurrection at birth. However, Siobhan was maturing; gaining confidence. She was also her mother's daughter and she really loved her father.

"He was meant to have a transplant to save him. To make him better. What have you done?"

"It was the right decision, Siobhan. When you are older you will understand."

Graham winced, scratched the small of his back and the top of his legs and shrunk, sadly not to nothing as he would have wished but certainly into insignificance. He hated being the cause of so much distress. He loved his daughter. Of course, he loved his wife and his son, when they let him but, somehow, he was outside that relationship. Outside everything he rued sadly. It would have been nice to get better but, well, Heather had a point. The liver was substandard; what if it hadn't worked?

"Yeah. But then I won't have a Dad."

It was if everything turned to stone. Cold, solid, fixed. The air slumped to the floor with Graham's hopes.

Heather's mouth opened but the words refused to come out – not us they muttered and stayed put.

"You told us that Dad was going to get better. You got us back from shopping as an emergency, you made us stay with Granny" (clearly she was a disease) "and all for nothing. It's not fair and you won't even tell us why."

"It would help to have the facts and then we can make an informed assessment of the situation" Archie ventured. An unlikely hero but timely. And Heather could never resist her son.

"The liver was fatty and what they call marginal which means it probably wouldn't have worked. It was too risky so we - your father and I - decided to wait for a better one."

This seemed to satisfy Archie who nodded sagely in grave agreement, bathing in his mother's glow of approbation. Siobhan however, wanted to probe further.

"What if there isn't a better one? How do you know it wouldn't work? Is that what they told you?"

"Yes" said Heather.

"Sort of" said Graham.

"Sort of?"

Really Graham, Heather's glare said as she grabbed the reins and steered out of danger. It was the doctors themselves who told them what the risks were. The consultant, a professor - a woman (so she must be right) who had got her chair (here Archie explained to Siobhan what that meant regardless of the fact that she already knew) from a most eminent Australian university, who was also the surgeon who would do the transplant was the one who had said so. Obviously she had recognised that she was speaking to intelligent people so she had said it as it was – no dumbing down. Not everyone would understand what she was saying, it would have to be spelled out to them, but not the Erikssons. She had spoken to them as equals and outlined the problems in such a way as to make them completely aware of the limitations of a substandard liver. Knowing also that Heather had had a medical training she had made it perfectly clear what they ought to do but, of course, she wasn't allowed to tell them how to act. Doctors were not allowed to make decisions like that – it was in the Patient's Charter. Heather and Professor Dennington had had a discussion about it.

"So she actually said that the liver would fail?"

Heather relaxed the reins a very little but continued to glare at Graham, warning him off any form of interruption. Unfortunately, Siobhan was observant.

"Dad? Is that what she said? That you shouldn't do it?"

"Your father made the decision in the best interests of the family – for his children" Heather answered.

"How do you know the next liver will be any better? What if it isn't? Will you turn that one down too?"

Of course there would be a better one; it was just a question of being patient Heather explained in her best 'you've no idea what you're talking about so I'll tell you' manner. Dad was 'stable' – yes, that was exactly what they had said - so time was on their side. Better to have the right liver than go through all the agony of a transplant only to find it hadn't worked and then have to go through the whole thing again. It wouldn't have been fair on Dad – we couldn't ask him to go through all that could we? What would it have done to him?

You had to hand it to Heather, Graham thought. She'd have made an amazing barrister. Sure enough, Siobhan had begun to feel guilty for even suggesting that her Dad should be put through so much and was descending from her standpoint faster than Icarus in high summer. But she was not going to hit earth without one last stab. Heather's genes were gaining strength, fledglings as yet but rapidly finding flight.

"How long will he have to wait?"

No one knew but at least they were all in this together. Weren't they? Heather said.

Were they? Siobhan had not finished.

"What if it's too late?"

Graham looked up at his daughter. Heather's eyes widened with innocence and purity to offset the disdain with which she answered. Whatever did Siobhan mean? Of course it wouldn't be too late; organs came up all the time and it would get even easier now that the law was changing and people had to opt out of donation instead of in. Child as she was, surely even Siobhan could see that? The decision they had made had been the right one and one day, when she was more mature and had some experience of life, Siobhan would realise that. Until then she must accept that her parents knew what was best for her - for them all and, especially, as a family.

And that was that. Discussion over as far as Heather was concerned. She knew she was right; Archie would agree with her as he always did – It was such a pity that Siobhan did not have his intellect – and Graham, well, Graham always agreed with her. They were completely united like that.

Betsy was irritated. Why didn't her father ever call her? Even when she asked him to? He must be back from the doctor by now but there had been no phone call, not even a missed one. She had been checking her phone all morning, especially when it was on silent when she was working. But the phone had not shivered or trilled or pinged or anything. In addition Betsy had a sore throat where her fingers had scraped and her teeth felt tainted in spite of several brushings and a small lake of mouth wash. At least her stomach muscles did not ache these days; probably getting used to it she mused with wry shame. And she had not put on a single gram; she had checked as she did every morning when she got up and went straight to the bathroom scales. Always in the morning though, never at night even if she was working lates. Her weight went up during the day and she knew that if she weighed at night it would depress her and she wouldn't be able to sleep.

Still no call from Dad. She found a quiet corner where she would be able to hear everything he said when, if, he answered and quick dialled his number. Miraculously he picked up before the ringing tone ended; he must have been awaiting her call.

"Dad. It's me. How'd it go?"

"Fast."

What was he talking about? Betsy tried to keep the impatience out of her voice. What had the doctor said? Done? She wanted to know exactly what had happened.

Sighing, as if about to repeat a long story already many times told, Ted embarked on the weary narrative of My Trip To The Doctor, as dull and pointless as the What I Did In My Holidays essay inflicted on school children every September. He had got there in plenty of time – yes, the taxi had arrived, early so he hadn't been quite ready but it was fine and the driver didn't mind. Nice chap… Get to the point, Dad. Well, he'd had to wait in the surgery but not too long which was a miracle and when he actually got to see the doctor – yes, a man (Betsy sighed with relief) who seemed to be in a terrible hurry. Apparently he only had ten minutes for each patient. Did Betsy know that quacks only had ten minutes for every patient? Oh, she did. Well, anyway, he asked me what was the matter and I told him. Yes, I told him about everything like you said I should, even the blood. Especially the blood. He wanted to know what colour it was! I mean, blood's red, who doesn't know that? Oh, I see. Well I told him it was bright red so it must be fresh blood if what you're saying is right. Which I'm sure it is. Then he wanted me to get up on his bed thing which was easier said than done from a wheelchair with half a leg. He had a prod of me belly and that was it. So I got down, yes, he did help me, then he said he was sending me to the hospital to see a gastro… onomer, gastronome, something like. Yes, gastroenterologist, that's the one. Within 2 weeks which seems quite quick which is good. Mikey at the pub waited three months for a hospital appointment.

Betsy said nothing in reply; she knew exactly why it was so quick and it had nothing to do with the efficiency of the NHS.

What did the doc say he thought it was?

Ted went quiet.

"Dad?"

"He was worried that it might be serious."

"Did he say why?"

"Cancer, darlin'."

Neither of them said anything. The C word. Out there now, silencing the air waves, numbing thought, tightening the throat, freezing the stomach. Betsy heard it all the time at work but this was different – this was her Dad.

"I expect he just wants the gastroenterologist to rule it out."

"Perhaps… We'll see."

"Dad? … Let me know as soon as you get the appointment and I'll go with you."

"That'd be great. Are you sure? I know how busy you are … Betsy?"

Yes Dad. Anything, Dad.

"Will you tell Lizzie?"

CHAPTER FOURTEEN

Agwe sat by Amber's bed in ICU and gave hearty thanks to Jah. Silently, eyes closed, smiling white somewhere inside his shaggy mane. Yeah, it wasn't very Rasta – the hospital, all that donation and transplant stuff but Amber was alive and man, he was glad. He had not left the hospital since she had been wheeled off into pre-prep and had hung around like a newly washed rug heavy with moisture taking forever to dry, all dripping limbs and fringe. Security had been called once by an elderly lady visiting her husband in male surgical; she had asserted that a disreputable man was following her: everywhere she went he was there too so he must be stalking her. However, by that time Agwe had become a familiar enough sight in the corridors, public areas, shop, men's toilets, stairwells and entrance lobby to be declared safe. Indeed, so often had he been seen that he was now expected and, like a male lion endlessly prowling out his territory, he appeared and reappeared with a regularity that was becoming quite comforting to resident staff. At one point the baristas in the café offered him a complimentary coffee as he passed: volunteers manning a hydration station during a marathon to keep the participant sustained as he ploughed his way to the finish line. Security grinned and nodded as he passed ... and passed ... and passed again. Amber was in theatre for the best part of six hours and he never sat down, not once. Walking was the only thing that stopped his legs shaking. He had bumped, literally, into Ann Williams on one of his circuits and she had hugged him. The elderly lady who saw them was about to report him for assault but his victim, a big woman who did not seem to be in the least distressed by the attack, appeared more than capable of defending her honour. When they parted she was smiling. Perhaps they were accomplices? In it together? But security had not taken her complaint seriously and the woman did not know what the world was coming to.

Now Agwe was finally confined to one place but his legs would not stop shaking so he jiggled them, up and down, remorselessly and silently as he kept vigil. Amber was so small. Not colourless as he had expected but yellow-grey pale, like a stain on the white bed linen. Her head and shoulders were propped up on pillows so that she looked as if she was sitting up except that her eyes were closed and nothing moved except the lines on the monitor glowing green and the trembling tubes in and out of her body. And that was only as a result of his own vibrating legs. She was an image in jaundiced monochrome, yellowing with age: a faded photograph, grainy, and bleeding white around the edges. Caught in the moment: a second for all eternity. But she was alive – the monitor said so – he kept checking and the specialist nurse assigned to her, just her, said she was doing fine and that he could sit there as long as he liked. ICU wasn't like ordinary wards with noise and light and visiting hours. It felt like a living museum or an art gallery where people talked in hushed tones, overawed by the exhibits. The technology was the seated curator watching, waiting, ready to pounce if hands went to touch or bodies ventured too close to the objects on display. So Agwe sat, outside time, not sure what to expect but determined to wait for it.

The thin-lipped, crumpled blue-clad surgeon had come to see him when Amber was being moved from theatre to ICU. She had said that the procedure had gone to plan and that the liver looked good on reperfusion (when the blood supply was restored – he had asked the nurse in ICU) and although it was a little fatty, the Professor (so she should know) was confident that it would be ok. Amber had been reasonably stable throughout, which was good, and he should try not to worry. The surgeon had seemed quite pleased, though it was hard to tell for sure, but he had hugged her anyway. Then he had rung Amber's mum, sent his love to the kids and now he was going to sit beside Amber for as long as it took. He wasn't going anywhere without her. It would not be the first time he had slept in a chair.

Fergus was frustrated. He had called Phoebe, left messages on her voicemail and even texted but the damn woman had not even bothered to get back to him. What was she playing at? Eventually he stopped ringing and resolved to seek her out, waylay the vixen in her lair, go to the bloody mountain itself. Not that she would know that. It would happen accidentally. He knew she had been called in to do an urgent transplant so there was no point in trying to catch her then, but that was yesterday. He had spent last night with the yoga-loving student nurse who while lithe and wonderfully flexible, had never stopped talking. Very distracting. Like having sex with a badly-tuned radio. Still, he felt invigorated so it was with vibrant intent that he sauntered down the central ground floor corridor and took the lift to the heady levels of senior management and the cupboard that Phoebe referred to as her office.

The briefest of knocks on the cupboard door – more of an impromptu tap than an announcement of arrival and certainly not a request for permission to enter – and he bowled straight in. At least it would force her to look up, if only to identify the intruder.

"Phoebe."

"Fergus."

Your move her look said and he considered which piece to play. Black King to white Queen. Sod the rules.

"New suit?"

Phoebe was disarmed.

"Yes. ... Do you like it?"

"Very much. It looks good with the blouse – silk? I thought so. The softness sets off the tailoring of the jacket. Pencil skirt?"

Phoebe stood up and he nodded with satisfaction. Excellent.

"Special occasion or just your impeccable style and good taste?" he enquired and took a seat opposite her, careful to keep the desk between them (not that there was much room to do anything else.) Phoebe liked to feel in control of her space; one had to be invited in, especially outside the bedroom.

"Not really. Just the usual ... Although I'm meeting Hugh Goldberg later this morning."

Ah, that was more like it. He knew something was up – Phoebe did not dress up for nothing and especially not for a nobody. Was it just routine or did she have a specific agenda? Oh, Hugh had asked to see her. Interesting. Did she have any idea what it was about? Well, she would find out soon enough but...

"Yes?"

"JA? Will you say anything?"

His phone began to clatter and shout in his trouser pocket so that he was forced to tip his body to one side to retrieve it, clamouring and calling. Damn. It was the air ambulance service.

"I have to take this" he apologised, standing up and heading to the door. "I'll call you."

It was hard to tell if she had even heard.

Professor Hugh Goldberg, illustrious (he begged to differ) Medical Director of one of the largest NHS Trusts in the country was not looking forward to his morning. But then he never did. His office was large, well lit, comfortably furnished and tastefully appointed. High at the front of one of the huge towers that comprised the heart of the hospital with a view right across the city into elusive freedom beyond, he would have loved to have time to sit, remove his half-moon glasses and stare the way his visitors did. What a marvellous view, you're so lucky, I'd never get any work done had largely replaced the more conventional thank you for your time, nice to see you, I won't keep you long sort of conversations that graced less rarefied work spaces. On the infrequent occasions when he had time to look up from his computer screen and out of the window he was transported into a lost lamented past. Cambridge. Hope. Idealism. Change. Narrow cobbled streets, mellow stone, desert boots, real ale, books, pens, paper and files, phones fixed to walls from which to make the weekly call home, sun on long days when all the girls were pretty (especially Penny) and wore cheesecloth. Even his own flame-coloured hair had reached his shoulders. He would have liked it there still but the Pre-Raphaelite look of his youth was singularly unbecoming on an aging Medical Director. So his curls were limited to the top of his head where they receded from his brow into a lively paprika party but he always wore bright red socks, as if to compensate for the loss. No wonder he was a hepatologist – it went with the colour.

There was a knock at the door – there always was – and his next appointment had arrived, just as his secretary had confirmed it would when they had gone through his schedule (how long was it since it had been called a diary and was a real book?) and shared a coffee. They drank it in her office, so much smaller and less salubrious than his own, so much more comfortable. Debbie swivelled from side to side in her chair – waist trimming exercise she said, so she'd fit into a wedding dress when the time came, while he slumped in a hard chair beside her like a badly put together crimson-tipped spider. Apart from when it ended, this was the best part of the day. Perhaps if he had married and had a daughter ... he wondered where Penny was now and if she still wore cheesecloth - that long floaty thing with the sleeves that went wide at the wrists like trumpets.

“Come in.”

Not Penny but Phoebe. Probably more what Penny might look like now, apart from the head. Smart, sharp, defined and neat, one slender line in cream and navy with those pointy shoes that had some connection to cats but for the life of him he had no idea why. The hair was dark and swept back into a sort of bun, like a croissant that went up the back of her head whereas Penny’s had been fair – strawberry-gold, loose and free. It blew over her face and invaded her eyes but she had never seemed to mind.

“Phoebe. Thank you for coming. Please…” he indicated a seat opposite on the other side of the desk. A gracious nod of the immaculately pinned croissant and she sat, legs together, knees regally central with feet a little to one side. “I know how busy you are”.

Another nod, not a hair out of place.

“I’ll get straight to the point if you don’t mind.” It was not a question. How uncharacteristically rude, thought Phoebe. It must be something serious. Well, wait until I tell him about JA.

“We’ve had a written complaint from a … Mrs Eriksson”. Here he glanced at his computer screen and then at a sheet of A4 before him. It was upside down so Phoebe could not read what it said. “It was addressed to the Head of the Trust who has passed it on to me as the Medical Director to deal with. Mrs Eriksson alleges that …”, here he referred to the document on the desk, “you were rude to her and have violated Patient Rights. … Her words.”

He looked up. Phoebe’s face was a blank. Impassive; shuttered. Only her mouth showed any reaction and had sliced itself into a single dark shard.

“Would you like to comment?”

Yes, she would, but she would take her time and choose her

words carefully. She contemplated her superior's blue blazer and recalcitrant curls. He would be wearing those ghastly grey crimplene trousers with the ridiculous red socks he always wore. A man in his position! As he waited, she watched him extricate a badly folded, un-ironed white cotton handkerchief from his blazer pocket and begin to wipe those pointless half-moon glasses which he had removed with the languor of a man about to fill a pipe. Tactical. He would wait for her to speak, as long as it took, and she would be forced to commit herself.

Yes... (should she call him Professor Goldberg?) Hugh, she knew exactly to what Mrs Eriksson was referring and it was, of course, absolute nonsense. Heather Eriksson was – this was not personal of course but merely stating the facts - bombastic, arrogant, entitled, ill-informed and aggressive. The Medical Director did realise that Heather Eriksson was not in fact the patient at all? The actual patient was her husband, the unfortunate Graham and, as Phoebe was sure the Medical Director was aware, if he had looked into the case, (he had) that the circumstances surrounding the recent debacle with the Erikssons were both ethically and medically complex.

"Heather Eriksson cannot bear to be challenged or contradicted" Phoebe concluded. "She has to be right and if she doesn't get her own way, she is one of those people who will resort to even the most underhand means to get what she wants."

"Is it wrong to want the best medical treatment for her husband?"

"No, of course not but..." for a moment Phoebe faltered, but not for long. "He was offered the best treatment available at the time. It was his choice – hers – to refuse."

"The liver was, as I understand it from your own documentation", here he casually replaced his glasses, shoved the handkerchief into a trouser pocket and only then glanced at the paper on the desk, "DCD marginal and fatty .... Their decision was not unreasonable."

"Not unreasonable? When so many people are desperate for donor organs? What gives him – them - the right to pick and choose? A chronic shortage of donor organs and he rejects one!"

So much for taking her time and choosing her words carefully. For a moment Phoebe was intensely annoyed – outraged – passionate. Fergus would have been astonished. Hugh Goldberg was unmoved. He continued to study the paper for a moment then looked up. He had not taken seriously the allegation of rudeness against their very own ice queen but then he had never before seen her quite so animated.

"Would you say that you were rude to her?"

"No. I was direct. ... On point. It's the only effective method of communication with someone like Heather Eriksson, whom I take it you have never met? A pity, because then we would not be having this discussion."

There, Phoebe thought, stick that in your pipe and smoke it.

Hugh Goldberg waited for a moment before he spoke – let Phoebe think she had the advantage then pull the pin from the grenade and throw.

"Why shouldn't Mr Eriksson still be top priority for a transplant?"

"Because he refused a liver."

"For very good reasons. I might well have done the same."

Boom.

Would you? his eyebrows asked as he peered over his glasses and studied the surgeon on the other side of the desk. Still perfectly coiffured, elegant and smart but she had crossed her legs and one pointy toed shoe was twitching up and down.

Fallout.

"It's a question of risk benefit ratios isn't it, Phoebe? A patient on the edge of life such as ..." he looked down at the document on the desk although he knew exactly what was written on it.

"Amber Kowalski, who accepted the organ, wants that life prolonged and will seize any opportunity to do so. Graham Eriksson is not facing imminent death but wants to improve the quality of his life. Outcomes from fatty livers, as we both know, are significantly worse. Can you blame – punish – someone for hesitating if they think they might compromise their current state of health?"

"But isn't he the one who is punishing people? All the other people on the list who are desperate for the kind of chance he refused? There are nowhere near enough cadaveric donors to meet the huge and growing demand and death on the waiting list is currently running at 15 – 20%. Try explaining to one of those patients and their families why a man, who refused one organ, is still at the top of the list for next one that becomes available – if he condescends to accept it. And if he doesn't, will he still be at the top of the list? Why should he have the luxury of choice?"

"Because he's not dying." Direct, but not rude, Phoebe – that's how it's done Hugh thought. It was wasted on her.

"But he might, in the future. He won't get any better without a transplant."

"That's a risk he knowingly takes. From what you say of his wife, I've no doubt they've weighed up the situation and investigated other options. Even if they haven't discussed it with you. Obviously in his condition the possibility of a living donor will have been considered – his wife for example, from what you say if she fitted the criteria – but we both know the risks involved with that. He's a father – of two children I believe?"

Phoebe would have liked to argue. "Teenagers" was her best effort.

"They still need both parents."

"The change in the law will improve the situation. When people have to opt out instead of in, there'll be more organs available so it doesn't matter if Graham Eriksson isn't at the top. He's stable – he can afford to wait."

"That's true, Phoebe. But by your own argument Graham Eriksson can also remain at the top of the list because of the increased opportunities for everyone else on it. However, this is hypothetical. It will take time for the change to take effect and in the meantime, we have to proceed with things as they are."

A moment of mutual reflection. Hugh was aware of passing time and the length of his schedule as discussed with Debbie that morning. He spoke.

"Who are we to make the decision to accept or refuse an imperfect liver or any other organ for a patient such as Graham Eriksson anyway?"

"Because we're the specialists. We know better."

"Do we?"

"Of course we do. We're the proven, recognised medical experts with the experience, training and knowledge. It puts us in a better position to assess risks and outcomes than anyone else. I've put my name to, and published numerous academic papers that testify to my skill and expertise. They more than qualify me to make the best decisions for my patients."

Hugh peered over the top of his glasses and scrutinised the tailored navy and cream animation in front of him. The crossed leg was now tapping the air as if to kick it into touch, the arms were folded across the tight, seamed chest and the earrings, large pearls which were no doubt real, he noticed, bounced energetically in support of her protestations. Look they said – listen to her – she's right - before they sank back into her earlobes with a shiver of indignation.

"How many of those papers have you actually written though?"

There, he had said it. He who had written more papers than he could recall without pain – perhaps he would still have Penny if he had written less. "We're qualified to assess, yes. To decide?

No. Ultimately it must be the patient's decision. Sometimes I think the hardest part of our job is knowing when not to intervene. We're only doctors."

Phoebe was genuinely shocked. Was Hugh Goldberg agreeing with Heather Eriksson?

He perceived her discomfort.

"I make it a point never to agree or disagree with people like the Erikssons. I simply weigh up the facts, present them, say it as it is – dispassionately – and then let the patient decide. If they ask me what I think, I'll tell them but I don't expect them to listen."

"Are you saying that Graham Eriksson should remain at the top of the list – a priority case?"

"On this occasion, yes. Had he rejected a sound liver I would, like you, want to see him moved down in terms of priority but he hasn't, so he won't be." His decision, over hers, and it was final. How would she take it? He could overlook the allegation of rudeness – Heather Eriksson would no doubt accept written confirmation of her husband's position at the top of the list as an apology in itself and, to be honest, he rather sympathised with Phoebe. It was a dilemma – their whole working life sometimes felt like a dilemma. He was also beginning to regret the comment about the papers she had not actually written, even if it was true.

"How about a cup of coffee, Phoebe?"

A peace offering. The schedule would have to wait. The first rule of successful management – don't fall out with people; you never know when you might need them – had served Hugh well thus far and he did not want to jinx the run. He inserted one lanky fingered hand into his mattress of curls and rolled them around thoughtfully as he attempted to lighten the mood. Perhaps some of their rosy colour would take the chill off the atmosphere.

Phoebe declined. She was preoccupied with the notion that

bloody Heather Eriksson would believe she had won. But it was a Pyrrhic victory. Every transplant was achieved on the back of someone else's tragedy and she thought of the fatty liver that she had so recently transplanted into Amber Kowalski. They had all complained about the state of the liver but at least it wasn't them who had died to provide it. She was glad that the family of the donor would never know that their sacrifice had been so criticised and even rejected as inferior.

"How is Amber Kowalski doing?" Hugh was asking. Hell, was he telepathic? Phoebe could at least answer that the transplant had gone well and that all the signs were for a successful outcome but ... there was something else she wanted to discuss with the Medical Director. It was of a delicate nature and she felt somewhat uncomfortable in bringing up the subject. However, in the interests of the hospital and good medical practice she felt she had no choice.

Now it was Hugh's turn to be surprised. It was never a good omen when he was referred to as The Medical Director. He sat back in his chair, tensed for the blow, feet flat on the floor, socks on red alert. Phoebe began to tell him about Jeremy Albright and the events of Theatre 4 when she had been required to perform 'an intervention.' Phoebe had learned something at least from her encounter with Hugh. The account was delivered dispassionately and politely. It took a while; no detail was omitted and Phoebe made it clear that everything she said could be verified and confirmed. And yet, Hugh found it hard to believe.

Was it really only lunchtime?

CHAPTER FIFTEEN

No one could say that Fergus was choosy. They did not have to be young or even pretty (although it helped), but he did prefer women who were natural. Make-up to enhance rather than remould, coloured, highlighted hair but done properly, with taste and preferably a professional touch. You could always tell when it was home-made – a block of colour, uniform, solid and unbroken, clashing with skin tone, desiccating and drying; the lamentable proclivity of an ageing woman without the means to feed her vanity and lack of confidence. The first sign of MDL as his father used to say, and he knew a thing or two about women. MDL - Mutton Dressed as Lamb he had explained sorrowfully to the boy Fergus during one of their walks together. No taste in that. A woman with the confidence to age without embarrassment or artifice was a glorious thing and well worth the pursuit. A woman such as Phoebe, Fergus thought and regretted that his father was not alive to witness the outcome of such sagacious advice. One of the most useful aspects of hospital life was that women could be seen without decoration, under stress: completely natural. Uniforms and scrubs did little to flatter but gave the discerning onlooker more than enough indication of the quality of body beneath. Not just in shape but density, flexibility and potential. Garments that fitted where they touched were like signposts and Fergus was adept at following their directions. Hair up under hats, necks revealed, cheekbones perching above masks, ears, wrists, waists clasped by plastic aprons, all spoke to him, an internal sat nav system around the human form.

Vikki Albright was no Phoebe. She had the advantage of youth of course, and was well-enough shaped, if a little lumpy around the hips, a sure sign of a woman who worried about her weight and probably a yo-yo dieter. On the scales every morning most likely, always watching what she ate and wanting more than she allowed herself. Doubtless a follower of fashionable easy-to -follow diets in weekly women's magazines which she would read then donate to the Imaging dept waiting room. JA probably did not know that she even bought them. Her head was encased in a golden helmet of Wagnerian proportions, an unbroken savannah of bottle-bright-blonde hair, straight, regimental, on duty. It glowed as a spotlight, a beacon for patients and radiographers alike. Useful for the cubby holes and corners of the imaging world Fergus mused; follow Vikki and you would never get lost. Odd though, that with a husband on the kind of salary that JA commanded she should be dyeing her own hair. Too frequently by the exhausted look of it and the complete absence of dark roots. Was JA a tight wad? He had never given that impression. More likely he had no idea that his wife dyed her hair and if anyone had asked would have said that she was a natural blonde – had always looked like that. Perhaps he thought the eyebrows were false? Pencilled in to be darker perhaps? And it did make Fergus speculate about their private life – surely JA must have seen her naked, even if just in the bath or shower? Unless she dyed her pubic hair? Or even better, had none. That made him smile and reinvigorated his appetite which, it had to be admitted, had hesitated once or twice.

Consequently Fergus found himself wandering nonchalantly into Imaging, file (empty) in hand, asking specifically for Vikki Albright. Did it have to be her? Couldn't someone else help? enquired the receptionist. Well, he had not the slightest doubt that she could (the lady pinked) but it was Vikki to whom he had been directed so he felt he must do as advised. She was busy?

Then he would be very happy to wait – would the receptionist (such an important role; the face of Imaging) like a coffee or something while he did so? He would be happy to oblige. That was very sweet of him (she pinked a little more) but she had just had one so, no thank you, but how nice to be asked. By a senior medic no less, an anaesthetist. She knew of course that Dr Crombie was a bit of a ladies' man – had quite a reputation actually – but no one could deny that he had such perfect manners. So rare these days. She would message Vikki whom she knew would be there as soon as she could. Oh, it was no trouble, no trouble at all. Happy to help and she ran her fingers through her natural to the point of anarchy hair and wished she was three stones lighter.

While anxious in his society, since marrying Jeremy, Vikki had become more accustomed to being in the company of senior medics although she did her best to avoid his Oxford friends. Out together she would grip her erudite husband's hand and never left his side. So devoted, so loyal everyone said, partly because she was joined to him at the hip but mainly because they had nothing else to say about her. She was a competent staff nurse and enjoyed the luxury of working part time even though there were no children at home. Jeremy was concentrating on his career, really getting himself established she told people; plenty of time for children later. Except that recently she had stopped mentioning the children. Jeremy's career was by now pretty well established and seemed to be taking care of itself as so often happened when you got to a certain stage in the NHS. Not to mention the private practice. It could be such a struggle to get to consultant but then the sweets of success tended to flow of themselves. They had the house in the right part of the city, the cars, the soft furnishings and occasionally an exotic, exclusive holiday. Nothing cliched though, however expensive. Whatever was required to convince people that they were used to having plenty of money and had always lived like that.

Fergus, therefore, was curious. Why did she dye her own hair? He had not met her socially so could not comment on her clothes outside the hospital – although he had plans in that direction. Nevertheless, there was sufficient enigma about her (or was it JA?) to make her worth cultivating. God knows he thought, there's precious little else. Phoebe – I'm only doing this for you.

So it was that Fergus found himself in the windowless world of Imaging, centred in the bowels of the hospital: dark, artificially illuminated, through which almost everyone seemed to pass at some stage: small intestine for an X-ray, large intestine for the CT and MRI big boys. Passages all to secret knowledge and hidden places. It was a labyrinth of doors and confines for changing, or seeking refuge, or watching, or manipulating machinery. Unholy cloisters where consultants sat in darkness studying monitors, scrolling down inner organs, analysing skeletons in cupboards. Solitary figures lit up only by reflected light like men in caves watching fires; medical troglodytes.

The invading anaesthetist did not have to wait long. Vikki was somewhat disconcerted to be told that Dr Crombie had made his way to Radiology specifically to see her. Her first reaction was to wonder what she had done wrong but she knew that was silly – there was no way she could have done anything. She had only met the man once, maybe twice when she had been with Jeremy and she had never worked with him so how could she have done something dreadful? Jeremy was right: she really should be more rational. She greeted Fergus rather too formally for comfort, which amused him.

"Please, call me Fergus" he gushed, smiling for all the wrong reasons. "I'm here to pick your brains if I may?"

Vikki's astonishment was almost endearing. No one had ever accused her of having a brain, never mind one worth picking and she was taken aback. Jeremy was the clever one.

"Well" she said and smiled back. "I'll do my best but are you sure it's me you want?"

"Oh, absolutely" Fergus replied with an intensity that made her shiver and she reached to her head to clutch at her hair as if it was a hand rail to prevent her from falling.

For a moment nothing was said while Fergus gazed at all that blondeness, mesmerised. She gazed back, hand still holding onto it.

"Light in the darkness" she heard Fergus murmur as if talking to himself. "Persephone in the Underworld." Then he appeared to pull himself together, shake off the poetic and assume a more business-like persona as he visibly tore his eyes from her hair and focused on her face, staring into her eyes. She really should look away, of course but, well, he seemed so intent. So, she stared back.

Fergus had a problem, a bit of a dilemma he said. He had been asked to anaesthetise a patient with learning difficulties who need to undergo a PTC. He had no idea whatsoever what was meant by a PTC and how he should go about it. Could Vikki – whom he knew by reputation was the best person with the most practical experience to consult – possibly help him? He would be so grateful.

"Oh, yes. That was easy. A PTC was simply a percutaneous trans hepatic cholangiogram."

Fergus marvelled. He couldn't even pronounce it, never mind understand it. Perhaps Vikki could elaborate? Why didn't they find somewhere quieter, away from the main thoroughfare and she could explain it to him properly? But he did not want to impose, if she was busy, as he knew she must be, someone of her importance in the department. He knew only too well how much senior medics and management depended on staff nurses – they were the backbone of the hospital; the system would fall apart without them. How he regretted that consultants so often failed to appreciate the importance of the nursing staff without whom they would be totally unable to function. At which point he noticed that Vikki looked away and he tucked the information into the 'interesting I wonder what it means' part of his brain for future consideration.

One minutely detailed explanation later of the process of injecting a contrast medium into a bile duct in the liver after which X -rays would be taken to identify the anatomy of the biliary tract, Fergus, who knew perfectly well what a PTC was and why it was used, professed eternal gratitude to the lovely Vikki. (He gazed at her hair again) If he could ever do anything in return she had only to say and, if it was alright with her, he would like to keep in contact in case he needed further advice, especially as the patient had special needs. She wouldn't mind? Wonderful. Thank you. She was the magnetic resonance of the Imaging Department... couldn't he encourage her to move into anaesthesiology? After he had gone, file (no longer empty) in hand, Vikki felt unusually energised. Even the receptionist seemed to regard her with more respect. Later, when she had Googled Persephone on her phone, Vikki blushed.

Betsy studied her phone. This was worse even than calling her father after he had seen the doctor that first time. To her surprise she had found Lizzy's number in her list of contacts, not that she had ever dialled it. Probably put there as one of those 'just in case only in an emergency' numbers in a moment of organisation and good sense; certainly not out of a desire to stay in touch. But she had promised Dad that she would tell her half-sister and so she would, warts and all. But she had to be civil. Calm. Pleasant – if possible, even though this was one of those heart-sink-bad patient moments which could drive even the most seasoned clinician to alcohol, industrial strength caffeine, nicotine, finger nails or, as in Betsy's case, chocolate. Already she had consumed an illegal Kit Kat from the vending machine which she secreted in her pocket after furtive purchase as she passed through the corridor. Not that anyone would have minded – Fergus would probably have been pleased – but it was Betsy who wanted to believe it was not there. Nor that she had eaten it and so craved more that she had retracked and bought two more for guilty consumption but only after the call had been made. That was the deal – ring, then reward.

She pressed the call sign and waited. Maybe no one would answer and she could leave a message...

"Lizzy? It's Betsy."

Silence.

Which of them would crack?

Betsy.

This wasn't easy so she would just say it as it was. She told her half-sister as succinctly as tight-lipped loathing would permit about their shared parent's ill health. No, the prognosis wasn't good but it was only right that Lizzy knew. Yes, Betsy would go with him to see the consultant and – here she was unable to suppress hostility – she would of course let know Lizzy know what happened. If that was what Lizzy wanted?

More silence.

Lizzy broke this time to make it clear to her older semi-sibling that yes, she did have a right to know, that she had just as much interest in their father as Betsy (even though she was a doctor) and that no one would be able to accuse her, the daughter of Ted's second and much-loved wife (who should have been his first choice and ergo, Betsy would not exist) that she had ever neglected her father or did not care. Regardless of what Betsy might say or think, Lizzy had just as much responsibility for her father (if not more) and she would be with him every step of the way. When was the appointment with the consultant? So soon? That was unfortunate. She absolutely would not be able to take time off work at such short notice to go with him; they were inundated at the moment. It was sale time in case Betsy hadn't noticed – doctors didn't seem to understand commerce and the real world. As the store manager she was indispensable – it was impossible just to walk away, even for a morning – but she would start to make arrangements for the future. Presumably there would be treatment? Chemo and radiotherapy and that sort of thing? Of course, Betsy would be able to go with him, wouldn't she? There was always another doctor or a nurse to take her place; the hospitals were full of them.

At least she hadn't started on about over staffing in the NHS Betsy thought afterwards as she broke into the third Kit Kat. If she had even so much as mentioned how she'd seen medics wandering around hospitals with nothing to do while patients were waiting there might have been a complete breakdown of relations. However, the truce had held – strained and exhausted but held – and Betsy had earned her chocolate. Maybe more – one of those family size bags of Revels would be nice. It would be fine if she didn't eat for a couple of days after to make up for it.

Amber was making excellent progress. So good in fact that she was to be moved from ICU to the ward, albeit in the high dependency section. Phoebe was delighted, not least because she felt vindicated and could not wait to let Hugh know that the transplant had been a success. She knew she was right and Hugh Goldberg would be forced to acknowledge that he was wrong, professorship, Medical Director, Cambridge graduate, red socks and all. She would have loved to tell the Erikssons – well, Heather – that they had turned down a perfectly acceptable liver. Sadly that would have been unprofessional but perhaps when she told Hugh – she would give it another twenty-four hours, just to be certain that all was well - he might somehow let that ghastly Eriksson woman know. But she doubted it.

Phoebe's satisfaction however, was nothing compared to Agwe's. He had switched into full rejoicing mode. Having sat beside Amber, who for so long had been the colour of her name thanks to her illness and the toxins stored in her body, it had been nothing less than a miracle as she had gradually changed from yellow to pink. A beautiful healthy rosy pink. And the whites of her eyes were white – no longer heavy and sallow as rancid butter. Her whole body turned from washed out to filled up; she glowed, her face was a blush of health and even her finger nails seemed to shine. It was if someone was painting them with ever deepening layers of colour until, he wondered, they might turn crimson. Against her new skin her hair was gold, like a halo. She was an almond tree coming into pink and white blossom after a long tedious winter. She gleamed. He beamed, hugged everyone, held her hand as gently as if incubating a flamingo egg and kept quiet at her bedside only with the greatest difficulty. At least his legs had stopped their relentless jiggling so that the tubes attached to the patient could heave a sigh of relief, settle and deliver their contents at a much more sedate, respectable pace. White water rafting was all very well, but not in a hospital thank you very much.

Amber spent much of the time asleep but when awake, chatted animatedly with Agwe who was thrilled. Even her voice seemed less pallid. The first thing she wanted to talk about was the children who, yes, would be able to see her when she was on the ward but not before – we don't want to frighten them with all this Agwe said, waving both arms expansively at the nest of machinery in which their mother was cradled. The second was the donor, to whom she, they, owed everything. Would it be possible to say thank you?

For Norma life was much the same, but forever changed. She's marvellous, isn't she coping well? everyone said as they watched her repeating the daily pattern of her Before life. What they could not see was that the woman who went about After was not the same person at all, but quite, quite different. She smiled and chatted, talked about the weather, said she was fine, thank you for asking, visited the same shops in the high street, although she bought less and hardly any food. She wore the same clothes – no reason to buy new ones – and all the time she was floating. Above. She looked down with amusement at herself, far below, marvelling at the movement and noise of a world in which she no longer belonged. Only when she was at home did she feel solid and tangible. Then she could feel things, touch them, notice light and dark, a change in temperature, smell the furniture polish she used every day, hear the hoover as she vacuumed the pristine floors. Food tasted of nothing; tea was merely wet and hot (when she did not forget to drink it), even if she put in sugar the way Alan had liked it. His pyjamas were still under his pillow – she checked every night before she went to sleep. Only one thing had changed. She had resurrected the abandoned window box outside the back door, cleaned it, painted it and filled it. It still sat on the ground but now looked up at her when she went to inspect its fledging contents and give it water. Winter pansies, small and struggling but doing their best to survive and flourish for the kind lady who had given them a chance. She smiled at them so they smiled back and endeavoured to grow, especially when she covered them at night with an old net curtain to prevent death by frost.

Norma often wondered what had happened to Alan's organs. Rosni had told her that the recipients would remain anonymous so she would not know who they were, just as they would not know the identity of their donor. Although she understood why, she wished it was not so. Alan – all of him – had belonged to her and while she had given him up freely and with love, she would have liked to know where he had gone, who he was with, what he was doing. In some ways he seemed to be more alive than she was.

CHAPTER SIXTEEN

When JA was called in the following morning to see Hugh Goldberg 'as soon as possible' he looked forward to their meeting. He and his Medical Director had a bond, a connection and Jeremy had good reason to believe that when Hugh and his bizarre matching hair and socks eventually left post, it would be he who assumed the mantle. We're Oxbridge men he told everyone, especially Vikki, all the time. Enough said. Hugh probably wanted to consult him about some senior management issue which was not for general consumption or about the forthcoming monthly morbidity and mortality (M&M) meeting of which Jeremy was the chair. So when he was informed that a complaint had been made about him by one of their own – a fellow surgeon - Phoebe Dennington – he was astounded. Then indignant and then, very, very angry. It was unfounded, outrageous, a complete fabrication and misinterpretation of events. If anything, it was she who was at fault. He had asked her to come in on an unusual procedure merely to observe, as a spectator, but she had taken it upon herself to intervene. He had thought she would find the experience instructive and informative so had been invited to watch - but she had taken over. It was unethical and rude. In fact, it was he who should be complaining about her because of her unwarranted interference which breached their codes of professional conduct and had discredited him the eyes of his team. Rather than create a fuss when she had so rudely elbowed him aside, he had chosen to be the better man and stand back. It was more important that the operation ran smoothly and had a successful outcome than he asserted his rights over a badly behaved, over-controlling transplant surgeon. Just who did she think she was?

Hugh listened, removed his glasses, rubbed them with his tie, replaced them, removed them again, peered through them to check for specks of non-existent dust, then put them back on and let Jeremy vent. He declined to answer the question that ended the diatribe but let the man draw breath and compose himself as best he could, perched as he was on the edge of a soft chair into which he would disappear if he leant back. It was so typical of Jeremy to automatically take up residence in the only armchair in the office.

Unfortunately, Hugh said, scrutinising a document on his desk, it appeared that after consultation with some of those who were present, Phoebe's complaint had been corroborated. Of course, he interjected, as Jeremy was about to begin again, his enquiries at this stage were preliminary and informal and he very much hoped that they would remain that way but Jeremy no doubt understood that he, Hugh, as the Medical Director, had a duty to follow up any form of staff grievance. Particularly among senior surgeons. He peered over his half-moon glasses as if looking for a star that had wandered off course and needed to be brought back into line. It was not hard to anticipate how Jeremy would respond but it would have been nice to be proved wrong.

Alas, he was right. The fault lay not with Jeremy but the incompetent registrars, the so-called assistant surgeons who would apparently have been out of their depth in an abattoir. Quite how they had qualified was a mystery to their lead surgeon who had no idea how he was supposed to meet targets and effect successful surgical outcomes without the help of capable, informed, intelligent assistants. They were supposed to have been trained. He did not expect in circumstances such as they had found themselves, which could happen to anyone at any time

– all part of the job – to have to assume an unscheduled teaching role to compensate for their woeful inadequacies and short comings. Successful surgery was about team work. Everyone had to pull their weight.

"Quite" said Hugh.

He wanted Jeremy to know that he had not spoken to everyone present – he had decided at this stage not to contact Betsy Jones and Fergus Crombie whom, he understood, had been the anaesthetists. There would be no point in talking to them, Jeremy asserted. If Betsy had been doing her job properly, she would have been focussed on the patient not the events around the table and anyway, she had had to call for back up to which was the only reason that Fergus had been there. Neither of them was in a position to comment or judge. All of which merely endorsed his point about teamwork depending on competent practitioners. He deeply resented the implications of Phoebe's utterly unjustified complaint about him and would fight it all the way, wherever it was headed. All. The. Way.

Only now did he sit back in the chair, all shots fired but still in possession of further ammunition if required.

It was not often that Hugh was perplexed. He liked Jeremy, and Phoebe. He also respected them. A clash such as this was potentially damaging and embarrassing for the hospital and something he wished to avoid but, at the same time, he had a responsibility to good practice, not to mention maintaining peaceful relations among his leading clinicians. Perhaps it would be best to leave it there he decided. Nothing in writing, just a general airing of discontent about an unfortunate series of events that was open to interpretation. Jeremy might have felt insecure but Phoebe, it had to be admitted, could be very dominant and was not known for her sensitivity. The reg who had struggled with the clamp was still learning and it had been an unexpected, demanding, stressful procedure that had caught everyone off balance. The patient was doing well – he had checked – and had been moved out of ICU to the Upper GI high dependency ward. No one had ever reported fault with Jeremy before plus, he appeared to be highly regarded in the medical world where, it could not be denied, that a PhD from Oxford really counted. Phoebe's professorship was more obscure and less salubrious, her ownership of all those research papers was spurious to say the least and she did have a most unfortunate manner. So terse. So cold. So unapproachable.

Yes. He would leave it there. File it away as regrettable but not worth making an issue of. However, he would not forget.

Amber's new state of pinkness was causing problems – all of them good. She would not keep still, would not stay in bed, rest or slow down. Only when Agwe threatened not to visit or let the children see her unless she paced herself did she begin to do as she was told by the medics, nurses, porter, cleaner and even the lady who manned the trolley-shop, whose menace to withhold supplies of the fresh fruit Amber craved proved, in the end, to be the most effective deterrent. The physiotherapists were overjoyed: a patient who wanted to exercise! In the end they were banned from more than one visit per day and Amber was restricted, on doctor's orders, to the ward corridors in which she padded up and down as if trying to keep up with her partner's previous serial pacing; a sort of pink and white lion cub in a nightdress. Now that it was she who commanded the remote control for her life and not her diseased liver, the button was pressed permanently on play. Sometimes she selected fast forward which usually ended up in her having to pause but she never chose the off button; sleep yes, but never shut down.

Opposite her in the ward was JA's patient whose tumour had caused so much hassle in theatre 4. She too was making a good recovery – which is more than could be said for the registrar who had had such conflict with the clamp who was unable to move his arm higher than his shoulder for a good twenty-four hours. However, it did prompt him to assess his own lamentable state of fitness and to send off to Amazon for a set of hand weights which he used at least twice. Amber claimed that her unbridled energy was the fault of this patient who turned out to have a name and was called Lesley. It was her encouragement that had done it. The first time Amber had managed to hobble unaided to the bathroom, Lesley had clapped and cheered, the applause had gone to Amber's head and now she could not stop. The staff nurse on duty at the time preferred not to tell them that they were both astral-planing on opiates and almost certainly hallucinating, but the damage was done. Amber had a partner in crime and would not be deterred.

Thus it was that she, initially, then supported by Agwe, launched concerted attacks on Ann Williams when she visited about being able to contact their donor to say thank you. Yes, they understood why anonymity was required and yes, all about privacy and the need for discretion but they had to do something – anything - to show their gratitude. There must be a way. Even if the donor's family did not want to have anything to do with them, they simply had to let them know how much it meant. The gift of life. It didn't get much bigger, did it? As Ann herself frequently referred to organ donation in this way, not to mention the national publicity campaign promoting it, she was in no position to argue so after initial resistance gave in. There was a way. But it was entirely dependent on the donor's family. Amber could write a letter and give it to Ann who would pass it on to the Recipient Coordinator at the donor hospital if – but only if – the donor family wanted to receive it. This would have to be established before any such letter was sent and yes, Ann would ring her colleague and find out, if only to get Amber off the subject. Now, please, could they discuss her medication and how she was planning to cope with the rigours of domestic life when she eventually went home?

It was inevitable that after the events in theatre 4, JA and Phoebe would both find themselves in the same place at the same time and equally inevitable, that it would be sooner rather than later. Unwelcome but unavoidable. The encounter occurred in HDU -the high dependency unit - in the no man's land between the beds of their respective patients. Both surgeons were doing ward rounds so escape was impossible because of their retinues, hanging on to their every word, witnesses all. Normally so quiet, this morning the area between Amber and Lesley was awash with trolleys, notes, a pair of registrars (including he of the clamp) the ward sister (juggling both consultants), assorted junior doctors and, lowest of the low, medical students hovering like flies around an open wound. Cannon fodder with stethoscopes and notebooks. Prepared but afraid least a question was fired at them that they could not answer. Those with Phoebe were undoubtably more frightened. She fought a fair fight but always hit her target whereas JA preferred to instruct and inform: safer as long as one was prepared to appear enraptured and made conspicuous notes.

"Make room for Professor Dennington" JA ordered his team. "Or she'll elbow you out of the way."

His reg (clamp man) gaped and became suddenly fascinated with the chart at the foot of Lesley's bed. A slight jostling for position took place as the two teams separated themselves. Phoebe and JA both leading from the front, stood at the end of their patient's beds directly facing their charges, shielded from each other by two crescents of bodies and minions.

Phoebe was pleased with Amber's progress and relieved that Agwe was not there in case he started hugging her again. However it was important for Amber to remember that she was only just out of ICU and still vulnerable, particularly to infection. It was early days yet, there was a still a risk of organ rejection so Amber needed to take care. A pause for Amber to absorb the importance of this message, a moment of silence, shattered by JA.

"Yet another complication for Dennington. God, you wouldn't want her operating on your pet hamster."

A casual laugh accompanied his comment from the opposite

side of the room; all geniality and malice. Phoebe said nothing but flushed crimson, Amber's exuberance evaporated and now she was glad that Agwe was not there to retaliate. He had sworn undying allegiance to Phoebe Dennington. The junior doctors to whom JA had addressed the remark were as ashen as Phoebe was red and Lesley was confused. Hadn't Professor Dennington been in on her surgery? Was she at risk? She would have liked to ask Mr Albright exactly what had been done to her but could not get a word in edgewise as he was now sharing her prognosis with the students who were ostentatiously making notes and pretending that they had not heard his rudeness. The ward sister was speechless, in itself an occasion which at any other time would have caused comment but in the light of this consultant warfare paled into insignificance. But only temporarily. When it was discussed throughout the hospital later, her silence would be used as a significant yardstick by which to assess JA's vindictiveness.

Phoebe led her entourage from the room without saying a word. She ignored JA, studiously avoiding his followers and most particularly, the clamp man reg, whose discomfort and embarrassment were pitiful to witness. Clearly Hugh Goldberg had spoken to JA who must now know all about her complaint. Well, she did not regret it, nor did she retract a single word. Nothing would induce her to acknowledge that Jeremy Albright PhD had even spoken, never mind maligned her professional and clinical ability in public, in front of staff and even patients for God's sake. Hugh would have to be made aware of it of course. That was her duty. She need not say anything to anyone else though. Hospital gossip, which spread faster than Covid 19 in a closed box, would see to that.

Once scandal arrived in the canteen, it was open season, gloves off, accessible to all. A feast of speculation, to be chewed over and savoured, spat out, spooned up and re-tasted, endless helpings to be sliced, dissected, examined, rolled around the tongue and the taste buds until swallowed and digested. Then regurgitated, a mother bird feeding her young. Life giving sustenance. From the canteen it spread exponentially across the hospital and beyond, through corridors, wards, offices, theatres, staff rooms, changing rooms and consulting rooms until, eventually, it found itself in the warm darkness of Imaging, where Vikki worked. She could not help but hear even though no one actually told her what had happened. It was in the walls, on the screens, in the air, pumping out of ventilation shafts. Floating in the steam of hot drinks, available at a price in the vending machine. Initial indications were invariably the same - something to do with the way that people suddenly quietened and looked away when she appeared, even at a distance; the way they over-smiled at her but said nothing and abruptly vanished or became preternaturally busy the nearer she approached. No one had to tell it her was to do with Jeremy. It always was. She knew that he was called Jack Ass, not that anyone had ever said so within her known hearing, but everyone had nicknames so it was no big deal. It was only to be expected that a man with his background and credentials would be resented and mocked – people were envious, felt threatened, had to make themselves feel better by putting down someone so much their superior. Generally, she took no notice. But this time it felt different. There was an atmosphere; hostility; an edge that she could not see but was in constant danger of falling over. Only she and her husband knew what he was capable of, but that was their secret – wasn't it?

A low profile under cover of Imaging department darkness and it took very little time for her to piece together the essence of what had occurred between her dearly beloved and the Ice Queen. Even allowing for exaggerations and embellishments it made troublesome listening. She made sure that she was permanently occupied and unavailable for comment or conversation for the rest of the day and went home as soon as her shift finished, not even stopping at Waitrose to get something for their dinner that evening. She had lost her appetite and Jeremy never noticed what food was on the table. Chances were that he wouldn't be hungry either.

He wasn't but that didn't help. Why hadn't she prepared a meal? He'd had a long day. A difficult day. Not that she ever seemed to notice or to care. Why was it all about her? She had no concept of the responsibilities he carried, the stress he worked under day in and day out. Was it too much to ask that she gave him some support – even just a little, once in a while? But no, she couldn't and she didn't – couldn't even cook a decent meal for her husband when he arrived home, to the house he paid for, to all the luxuries and comfort that she enjoyed because he had studied and worked so hard and which she simply didn't appreciate. She was a selfish, stupid cow and he didn't know why he'd married her. Oh, yes, wait a minute. Now he remembered. She'd said she was pregnant and it was only after the wedding that she'd miraculously lost the baby. The pick of all the girls at med school and Oxford and he'd chosen her. God, he was a fool, but at least he was not ignorant and uneducated, overweight and stupid like her. Bovine. Not that she would know what that meant. She was not good enough to lick his shoes – but she was still going to. Now. If she didn't kneel down, he would make her and as her golden helmet hair fell over his feet when she kissed them, he lifted one and pushed it into her face.

When Phoebe rang, Fergus was surprised. Delighted. Then uncharacteristically nervous. Why was she calling him? He always called her – it was one of those tacit understandings about which so much of their relationship was based. If indeed it could be called a relationship. Perhaps that was why she always left him wanting more? Christ, answer the phone, do the analysis later he told himself and picked up. Literally. He was at home after a busy day, some in the air ambulance but most in the refined environs of the Firtrees, the private hospital in the leafy suburbs, where they were dealing with the post-Christmas rush. All those gift vouchers for surgical cosmetic enhancements under the tree had now to be fulfilled. Numbers of breast enlargements were steady but this year they had seen a huge rise in vulvoplasties which had taken them by surprise; they had anticipated an increased demand for butt implants thanks to the Kardashians, but the designer vagina was a surging new trend and added welcome variety to their lists. God alone knew what would be next but rest assured, he and his surgical colleague had agreed, they would be ready to meet every new challenge head on. Now he was in his kitchen, pouring a glass of red wine and the mobile was on the counter beside him. Thank God he never went far without it.

"Phoebe." Don't sound surprised. Or too eager. Pleased but not overwhelmed. "What can I do you for?" Damn. Too flippant. Cheap. He hoped she wouldn't notice.

She didn't.

Could she see him? There was something she wanted to discuss.

Of course, yes, as soon as she liked. Now if she wanted. He had just opened a bottle of wine – white, dry, chilled, just the way she liked it. A Chablis actually – her preferred tipple. Perfect timing. Yes, he'd see her very soon...was everything alright? But she did not reply having not even heard his question because she had ended the call and was already picking up her car keys and her handbag and letting herself out of her immaculate white hallway.

Fergus went to the fridge and selected one of the bottles of Chablis that he always kept, just in case. He flung his glass of red down his throat, sealed the bottle, put it away and rinsed out his glass before finding another matching glass from the cupboard. He dried the wet one, polished the one intended for Phoebe with the tea towel, flung everything out of place on the kitchen surfaces into the dishwasher or the fridge then wondered anew what the hell was happening.

He soon found out.

"JA said that?"

Phoebe nodded. She had not yet touched her wine but now sipped at it with lips clenched so tight that Fergus wondered how she would be able to get any of it in her mouth.

"On the ward?"

"No. On HDU!"

"In front of everyone?… Patients?" it was rare that Fergus was shocked. Surprised – often. Amused – even more often, but not this time.

"What did you do?" Probably not the right question but it just came out.

"Nothing."

"Good girl."

Phoebe smiled. "I wanted to kill him."

"Oh, we can do better than that, Phoebs." Fergus raised his glass. "To revenge" he said. "Cheers".

"No. To justice" said Phoebe, opening her mouth just enough to let in the wine.

CHAPTER SEVENTEEN

Ted's appointment with the consultant had come through and in compliance with the two week deadline for suspected cancer cases was scheduled for just one day later. He rang Betsy who knew at once on seeing the identity of the caller what it must be and had already started planning by the time she picked up. She would be there, of course she would be there. No, they wouldn't be able to get Ted's wheelchair in her car but there'd be one at the hospital they could use so, yes, he could still roll up in a Mercedes if that's what he wanted. They both knew it was not so much his arrival at the hospital that mattered to him but his departure from the sheltered accommodation. Pointless to ask then, Betsy thought, whether he had told anyone there about his condition (he refused to call it an illness). Clearly he hadn't. How he would explain her sudden arrival and protracted stay she did not know and cared less. Her immediate problem was logistical. Compassionate leave could be arranged but only if and when the consultant had made a diagnosis; until then she would have to arrange cover for all her anaesthetic duties. She got straight onto the phone to Fergus – not the landline but his mobile. Time was of the essence as Phoebe Dennington would say.

"Allow me..." Fergus was already topping up Phoebe's glass when his phone went off, bouncing eagerly on the kitchen work top like a spoilt child crying for attention. Fergus leant away from sommelier duties towards the phone and saw who was calling.

"Damn. I've got to take this. Sorry. Won't be a minute."

Just time to pick up his own glass and head out of the kitchen into the hall where, with the door closed, he would not be overheard. Not that Phoebe would listen.

"Hi."

As usual he avoided saying her name.

"What can I do you for?"

Predictably Betsy giggled. Then she was serious and explained why she was calling. Yes, Fergus would cover for her. No problem. Several procedures scheduled in theatre with Phoebe Dennington? Again, no problem, leave it to him. He would let her know and sort out all the admin. What mattered was Ted; she had to be there for her father that was a given; family came first. Not having any family of his own to prioritise or be concerned about, Fergus was all calmness and sanguinity so that Betsy marvelled at his understanding and strength. She did not know what she would do without him and made the mistake of saying so. How could she ever thank him? Oh, he'd think of a way he replied and, predictably, she giggled again. Then he became kind and asked if she was okay.

"Not really. I'm as sure as I can be that it's advanced – maybe stage 4 already. I'm frightened I'm going to lose him, Fergus."

"There's no point in speculating. See the consultant and then react... Does Lizzie know about the appointment?"

Tactical; move her off the emotion and back onto the pragmatic. It was a brilliant diversion and he congratulated himself as her angst became fury directed towards her self-centred, egocentric half-sister who put a shop before her own father. Until it became boring.

"When are you going north?"

First thing in the morning. Was there any chance of them meeting up before she went – she could stay at his place overnight and travel north from there if he liked? Oh, he would, he would have liked to very much but alas, he was already committed. Stupidly he had agreed to do the anaesthetic for a breast enlargement (how much better you'd look with one he thought, remembering the FY1 in the tight blouse) – private – a last minute thing but Fergus had said he would be there, short notice as it was. He'd made a commitment – couldn't let people down – he knew Betsy would understand. He was about to head off there now - she had only just caught him.

If only he had known. Never mind, they would stay in touch and he was there for her; would be thinking of her. She was not to worry about anything at the Birmingham end where everything would be taken care of – he would see to it. Now, she was to travel safely; let him know when she got to Newcastle and there was to be no racing up the road and taking risks for the sake of arriving just a few minutes earlier. Anyway, it might be better that she got a good night's sleep before her journey ... At which point she giggled once more and he had the satisfaction of knowing that their call had ended with a smile.

He was just in time to replenish Phoebe's glass and suggest that she stayed the night.

The following morning Vikki headed into work earlier than usual. She left Jeremy brooding in the kitchen over his coffee and was glad to arrive unnoticed to sink into the dim, closed quietness of Imaging without seeing anybody. Or rather, without them seeing her. Her face was fine. Jeremy was good that way, he never left marks, not where they could be seen, but she wore her shame and mortification like bonfires beneath her foundation and was convinced that they burned as fierce as they felt and that everyone would notice. They did not, but put her reticence down to being aloof and a bit of a snob – just because she's married to a consultant; thinks she's better than us; only a staff nurse for God's sake, and nothing special to look at. What does he see in her?

Jeremy's thoughts were focussed on more important matters. His meeting with Hugh Goldberg had not only been disconcerting but he was incensed. Incandescent. He was glad that Vikki had gone out early – she was so irritating – and he could concentrate on how he would address the problem of Phoebe Dennington. Her accusations against him were intolerable but could be damaging. It was essential that Hugh did not take them seriously so something had to be done to discredit her. It was a question of what, when and how. She was a competent surgeon so unlikely to foul up in theatre, especially now, when she must know she was under scrutiny so he would have to find another way. Not for nothing did he have a PhD; strategic thinking was his speciality. He had to implement something subtle, credible, founded in fact (however spurious) but within the existing framework of hospital good practice. It had to be plausible but not directly related or attributable to him ... and he had an idea. Part of his job was to lead for clinical governance for surgery. He chaired the Morbidity and Mortality meetings every month where all deaths and complications had to be discussed and for years, he had been storing all the data from those meetings in files – one for each of his colleagues. It had been his personal and private initiative of course, done purely for administrative and organisational reasons. One never knew when such information might be required – like bank statements he stored them for seven years at least. Purely for reference; a historical record. The cases had already been discussed in M&M meetings which were open forums where learning points were raised, discussed and implemented. After which it was universally considered 'case closed' - but why not 'reopen' them where Dennington was concerned ... from 'a patient safety perspective'? What better way to lobby senior colleagues against her?

Infinitely cheered Jeremy abandoned his coffee, breakfast dishes and the kitchen – housework was Vikki's job – and headed off to work.

Ted's appointment with the consultant was mid-afternoon so after an early start, Betsy arrived in North Shields in time for a cup of tea but no sandwich, thank you, she'd had something on the way. She hadn't and Ted knew she hadn't but said nothing. Neither had he. His appetite seemed to have been flushed away with the blood and the less he ate, the less time he would have to spend crouched over the toilet bowl, half leg akimbo. He was relieved that Kelli, who came in to clean twice a week, didn't seem to have noticed anything untoward. He had been careful to wipe down the wall beside the toilet and its seat but then Kelli missed cobwebs hanging like hammocks from the kitchen ceiling, hoovered in rigid lines only where the wheels of his chair had made tracks across the carpet and did not believe in antibiotic sprays – bad for the environment she said. That was why she left the cobwebs. Nature's engineering – beautiful – a crime to spoil them and Ted never had flies or insects, did he? There! And no chemicals involved. A quick once over with a dry duster was plenty, so she briefly stirred the air in the flat and then let it simmer, cool and retire. Ted had lived in the flat for years and had inherited the floor coverings from the previous (deceased) owner. They had been included in the purchase price with no extra charge for wear, tear and stains. Betsy and Lizzie had uncharacteristically been in agreement about the need to steam clean the carpets but Ted had refused – what was the point when his chair would be all over them and he was never going to walk barefoot? They had had the carpets cleaned anyway, as well as replaced in the bathroom and kitchen with vinyl flooring. They might need to use the facilities. Nor would he change the nets, even after the walls had been painted and magnolia splashes festooned them like mouse droppings. There was no way they were coming down, not even when the decorators were in. Fecking nosy neighbours. Ted had moaned and complained about the expense and the nuisance of the new flooring but now, clearing up after his own bloody ablutions splashed all over the bathroom, he had to concede that it was useful. Not that he could ever tell them why.

Staying with her father was not easy but at least Lizzie was not there. Yet. Betsy would have to sleep in the living room on the too short to lie down properly sofa but with a pillow at one end she could swing her legs onto the floor and stretch out enough for a few hours unbroken sleep. Then she could curl up foetal style and hopefully sleep the rest of the night. It would only take a few minutes to unravel herself and get feeling back into the lower half of her body. This discomfort was nothing though in comparison to the temperature of the flat. It was tropical-Saharan, but without sand or wind. The air was old and tired like Ted; it felt as if it had been there a long, long time and had become agoraphobic. It shuffled around the small space unshaven, in old slippers and a saggy dressing gown in need of a wash, never fully opening the curtains or picking up its pace. Like Ted it smelt stale and was yellow at the edges. Two old books, musty and unopened.

They arrived early. Betsy advised against it; Ted's belief that the sooner they got there, the sooner it would be done, would not work. Believe me (he didn't), Betsy knew. They were at the mercy of the appointment system and the consultant's time which hardly ever ran to schedule. The fact that Ted was disabled made no difference – it was a hospital. She had warned him about the procedures that he would have to undergo before the appointment itself but he was still indignant. An enema? With the state of his bowels? Shit. Which at least made them laugh although the flexible sigmoidoscopy that followed was less amusing. Ted thought he had seen it all after his amputation but the vision of his inner self in colour on a large flat screen was repulsive and no, he did not want to look. Besides, he hadn't got his glasses. Betsy however did look and mourned the dimensions of the tumour on display. She was shocked both at its size and the fact that it was her father's – inside his body, her Dad, who'd always been there. She watched as a sample – so small in comparison to its host – was removed for biopsy. They would not know the result for a few days but she was a doctor; she did not have to guess.

It was no surprise when the consultant said that the likely diagnosis was cancer. Of course, he could not be sure until after the biopsy blood tests and CT scan results, which would help them assess the stage of the tumour and treatment options. Chemotherapy would probably be needed either before or after the surgery, depending on what the scan turned up. Turned up! Ted thought it sounded like an unexpected visitor on his doorstep, a forgotten relative, a lost key, the prodigal son. Or daughter. Bloody ridiculous phrase. But there was little doubt that Ted's book would need to be opened – surgery, yes - after which a stoma bag would almost certainly be necessary. At which point Ted, who had kept his thoughts to himself, finally spoke. Loudly. A stoma bag! Betsy thought he did not understand what had been said so began to explain but Ted turned on her, livid. He knew perfectly well what it was, but was damned if he was going to have one. Assurances that it would most likely be a temporary arrangement did nothing to console or appease. He had been purged and emptied, invaded, prodded, poked and photographed – and now they were talking about cutting him open, taking him apart and putting him back together with a plastic bag. And Betsy was just a bad as the consultant, who he knew was only doing his job, but it was unacceptable. He was a human being, not a piece of meat or an old car. And if he could have stormed out, he would, but he was confined to a fecking wheelchair.

After his departure in a flurry of circles and high dudgeon Betsy talked with the consultant. No prognosis was possible, obviously, until the CT came back but it was clear to them both that it was a sizeable mass and that the cancer was advanced. The consultant would not commit himself as to stage, but Betsy was a doctor – no doubt she could draw her own conclusions.

They would meet again soon but, in the meantime, perhaps she should encourage the family to spend quality time with him.

“Lizzie needs to know” she said as she pushed her father along the wide central corridor towards the atrium entrance.

“Know what?”

“That we’ve seen the consultant”. Betsy was glib. Ted did not believe her for a moment.

Vikki knew what was being said about her husband – it was impossible not to. Everyone was talking about it – and would do so until some new scandal usurped it – even (especially) in the dim, dark corners of Imaging. It occurred to her that this was deliberate – she was meant not to overhear exactly, but to know. People were too polite and pleasant. The receptionist was particularly attentive which was a dead giveaway. So when Fergus Crombie appeared on the horizon like a late dawn one afternoon, casting rays of light across the darkness, she was surprised and grateful. After he had sought her out that one time, she had never expected to see him again other than perhaps in passing in the canteen or a staff room, not that she ever went to either at present. The Albrights did not mix socially – Jeremy was very particular about the hospital company they kept; no-one below senior management was even considered appropriate and even then, it was always away from home, off the premises, in groups. Often he went alone telling his wife that it would just be all medical talk that she wouldn’t understand and she’d only be bored so she stayed behind doing housework that she had already done. However, she did watch TV, all the programmes that Jeremy hated and gorged on crisps and chocolate, putting the empty bags and wrappers in the outside bin so that he wouldn’t know. Sometimes she went for a walk, not far, but out of bounds, worrying all the time that he would see her or find out but then not caring. How could he possibly know? Not unless he was following her and she knew he wasn’t because she had watched him drive away. She had waved but he did not seem to have noticed.

Fergus wanted to discuss the way he should handle the special needs patient he had told her about – the one who required the PTC. Vikki had been so helpful, had explained everything so succinctly, he knew that she was the best person to advise him. All in the interests of patient care of course; he wanted to do his best for this particular patient and hoped ...a pause, slight hesitation ... that she did not mind him descending on her like this? She was busy, he knew, but ...

Thank goodness they were not in the brightly lit reception area peopled by patients and staff, all watching and listening. She could flush with heat, unseen, even by Dr Crombie. Fergus, as he had insisted that she call him. He had come specifically to seek her out, to ask her advice and she was touched. Flattered. She would be happy to help in any way she could – yes, perhaps they could meet to discuss it in more detail, if that was what he wanted ... Oh, he did. Very much. Then he had reached out and softly, reverently, like a silk merchant examining the finest most expensive cloth, had picked up a skein of her hair, and stood, holding it out like a ray of light, gazing at it. Said not a word but just looked. Felt the heat from her body, smelled her longing. This was too easy he rued, but there might be some fun in it.

"I shall call you Rapunzel" he whispered, so quietly she was not sure if he had even spoken. But she felt every feather touch of his fingers as they trickled down her spine.

Jeremy was having a good day. Profitable. Valuable. Enjoyable even. Phoebe Dennington was out at a meeting somewhere or other, something organ donation related which was disappointing in that he would not meet her on a ward round and be able to pass comment, but did mean that he had a clear run for the launch of his campaign against her. Meticulous examination of her clinical governance records had thrown up an excellent opportunity that although it had not increased his pulse rate, had made him smile. Some months ago, she had been involved in a poor choice of donor in a recipient who had had a subsequent primary non-function of their new liver. A traction injury in the donor artery had led to a hepatic artery thrombosis in the recipient which had required dissection and repair during a Whipple's operation. The surgeon had called Phoebe who had interrupted the procedure to carry out the repair then gone back and completed the operation. Clearly, she had form – the way she had hijacked his own procedure in theatre 4 was clearly just another example of the way she interfered and crossed clinical boundaries. Compromised safety; jeopardised successful surgical outcomes. Just why was a liver transplant surgeon doing Whipple's operations? Jeremy wanted to know. It was a legitimate question in the interests of patient safety and one that he had a duty of care to investigate; he and all those whom he made aware of it. And that was not all. Dennington was found to be remiss in other ways, most disturbingly where even less serious procedures were involved. Another patient had suffered from a leak after a lap chole (the removal of a retained stone in the common bile duct resolved the issue, but even so) which she had performed. A relatively simple, minor procedure which she had fouled up and which showed, most alarmingly, that she lacked concentration and rigour even in small cases. The woman was a menace. A danger. JA's smile spread across his face, but not quite as far as his eyes as he headed towards the staff room and the first of those whom he would be consulting about his concerns. As he walked, he put in a call to Hugh's office and made an appointment to see him at his earliest convenience.

CHAPTER EIGHTEEN

Amber and Agwe had agonised, debated, disagreed, agonised some more and finally decided to keep their letter simple and direct; to say exactly what they felt. Not knowing the identity or even the sex of the person? people? they were writing to made it more difficult and neither of them was used to writing anything, never mind letters. It had been a struggle even to find writing paper – 'no one uses it these days chick' – but Agwe was not to be overcome and took his lion's mane into every department store and stationers he could find in the city centre until Amber had the bright idea of trying the hospital shop where they found both paper and matching envelopes. Then she made a fuss about what she was to write it with. No, a biro would not do. One of those gel ink things would be best, but not a felt pen – try the hospital shop first this time.

Then it was done but what should they put on the envelope? And if they left it blank, how did they know it would get to the right person? It might get lost or mislaid or forgotten in spite of what Ann Williams promised. In the end they resorted to a Whom it May Concern from a Grateful Organ Recipient c/o The Organ Donation Coordinator. Ann would not even tell them which hospital to which it would be sent, if they were sure that was what they wanted?

"We only want to say thank you" Amber insisted with her resurging health and increasingly loud energy. The nursing staff were pressing for her to be moved from HDU into the ordinary ward where she could be spread more thinly. Her body showed no signs whatsoever of rejecting the new liver which appeared to have taken up residence within her as if to the manor born. Very comfortable thank you, settling in well, no complaints and looking to stay. Nice neighbours – very friendly, especially liked the pancreas next door, excellent blood supply and already looking at a long-term lease. Might even purchase.

"You will send it, won't you?" Agwe shook his mane. Ann caved in and agreed. Yes, yes, she would send it.

"Today?" asked the mane.

"Yes. Today. Slow down, Amber. It's meant to be physiotherapy, not qualifying for the SAS."

In Newcastle the rain was trying to be snow. Ted and Betsy were back at the flat, the Mercedes parked outside on the quiet street where all the neighbours could get as clear a view of it as their nets permitted. Net curtains all very much whiter than Ted's Betsy had noticed before she returned her gaze to the interior of the dismal front room in which they were sitting, waiting for Lizzie. Ted was out of his wheelchair and enthroned in a once dark brown, velour, high backed armchair, now muddy pond brown on the arms where the pile had been crushed and rubbed over the years. He looked like a damaged mannequin sitting on the lap of an ancient teddy bear, one leg short of a body, yellow with age where he had been over exposed to the sun and worn by the weather. Perhaps he had been forgotten and left outside for too long by a careless child-owner who had only recently rediscovered him, brought him indoors and put him by the fire to dry. Certainly he was beside the fire – a two bar electric fake coal with a red shimmer affair placed in the equally fake fireplace in the centre of the wall, fighting for attention with the large TV screen at its side. Ted's chair was angled towards the screen. His seat sat in solitary splendour to allow room for his wheelchair which hovered at his side like a sycophantic aide. Betsy perched on the edge of the sofa/bed, her duvet and pillow hidden behind it and waited. They were silent, listening for the doorbell through the snow wannabe as if this would somehow make the situation softer, more appealing, less tearful.

It never rang. Lizzie let herself in. Blonde, petite, as slender as her sister but with a more hearty appetite, she was just the same as when Betsy had last seen her... when? Years ago. At her step mother's funeral probably. She was even wearing the same black but the clothes were different - faux fur, tingled with raindrops which shone in the light of the electric bars, a silk scarf that poured from her neck as she unwrapped herself, black tights, black shoes, fitted sleeveless black dress under a short three quarter length sleeved jacket. Very smart, very tailored, very manageress. Very Lizzie.

"He's just as much my father as yours" she said by way of greeting and sat down, in the wheelchair.

"How're you Dad? Is she looking after you?"

"Hello darlin'. Yes." Ted angled one thin cheek in the direction of his younger daughter who leant forward to give it a quick kiss then sat back, checking first that the brakes were on so that she was not propelled backwards towards the kitchen where Betsy was now lurking.

"D'you want sugar?" The older sibling called, knowing how it would annoy the younger who had never taken sugar in tea in her life. No reply so Betsy heaped in a couple of spoonfuls.

"We saw the consultant today" she said as she reappeared with a tray. As if I didn't know Lizzie glared. She had come straight from work (as if they couldn't see by the way she was dressed) – taken time out of a busy day because this was important so could they cut the crap and get to the point? What did he say? Always the assumption that a consultant was a man Betsy thought, or was it just a jibe at her? She watched Lizzie grimace as she sipped the tea but say nothing, then carefully place the mug out of reach by the fake fire which shed its orange glow over it as if trying to set it alight.

Betsy described what had happened and what had been said. Just as she got to the part of proposed treatment depending on CT results, Ted put up a bony hand as if to stop traffic.

"I don't care about the results."

They looked at him.

"I'm not having treatment."

"What?"

Even he noticed, with a wry smile, that both his girls had spoken simultaneously, possibly the first thing they had ever done together apart from fight.

"You can't do that!" Betsy said.

"Can he do that?" Lizzie asked Betsy.

"Yes, he can. And he will" Ted announced. "I've made up me mind. There's no point."

What did he mean, no point? Of course there was a point! Betsy the daughter then, almost immediately, Betsy the doctor, the professional. The consultant. To tell him how it would be without treatment. The pain, the discomfort - and that was just the beginning. It would not be a sudden death but drawn out over days, maybe weeks. The pain could be controlled but what if he couldn't swallow and had to have suppositories given rectally? What if he was in pain but unable to tell anyone during the inevitable period of withdrawal before death? Confusion, agitation and even hallucinations were to be expected, not knowing who and where you were and who those around you were. Treatment was essential – while there was a chance of life, he should take it. It was madness not to. What about her - and Lizzie? Even if he didn't want treatment for himself, he should do it for them.

"Why?"

The rain, which had not become snow so was hammering

against the window in frustration was the only sound in the room. Ted examined his children - and smiled. Then he spoke, as softly as a winter dawn.

"You're good girls but selfish. Why would I want to have all that chemotherapy and radiotherapy stuff? Let someone cut me open and mess about with me insides? I've had me life so what's the point? You girls have your own lives, which is the way it should be, but mine's over and there's nothing much left for me to live for. Don't argue. You know it's true. And you know" – this to Betsy – "that if the cancer doesn't get me, the treatment will. No. I've made up me mind. I don't give a feck what the consultant and the scan say, I'm not having treatment. And that's an end of it. Now bugger this tea, I want a proper drink. Not scotch but Irish; Jameson's. There's a bottle in the cupboard under the sink and you know where the glasses are. If I've decided not to have treatment and be drunk for the rest of my life – which I very well may do - that's my choice."

"But it's his choice, Betsy." Fergus heard himself say her name out loud and marvelled at its ugliness. "It's his life."

"His death you mean."

"That too."

"What are you saying? He has to have treatment. As long as there's a chance of life he must take it."

"Why?"

"Fergus! That's what he said."

"It's a good question."

"It's a ridiculous question. No one chooses death, especially not a death like that. I told him what it would be like but he completely ignored me."

Fergus was silent at the end of the phone. He could just imagine what Betsy had said, and how, and felt rather sorry for her father. She had called him on the mobile and when, at first, he had not picked up, had rung and rung and rung so that eventually he had given in and taken the call. She hadn't even given him time to make an excuse for not answering before she was off, hysterical, banging on about her father's unreasonable, selfish, bloody-mindedness.

"What does your sister say?"

"Half-sister. She agrees with me."

"Really?"

"Yes. Dad was surprised."

"What? That she wanted him to stay alive or that the two of you had agreed on something?"

Now it was Betsy who was quiet. This was not the reaction she was looking for, not from Fergus. What was the matter with him? He was a doctor; of course he would want to prolong life, especially the life of someone so dear to the woman he loved. Yet he seemed to be siding with her father, whom he'd never even met.

Then it was as if Fergus had heard her thinking.

"I know I've never met him, but from what you've said, he's nobody's fool. He's certainly capable, from what you've said, of making up his own mind. He's opted for quality, not quantity of life. You can't blame him. What is he – seventies?"

He was younger: late sixties. But it made no difference. Ted was her father, not a statistic. If he opted for surgery and chemo there was every reason to suppose that he might have a good few years yet.

"You don't know that. You haven't had the scan results yet. And what about the quality of his life immediately after surgery – if it worked – and the effects of the chemo? Have you told your sister what that does? Not just the sickness and the hair loss but the fatigue, the compromised immunity and all the other possible side effects including sepsis, which in itself might cause death."

No reply from North Shields. Fergus pushed the scalpel in deeper.

"If it was me, I'd probably do the same. He's on his own, is confined to a wheelchair, hardly ever sees his children – no, don't argue; you know it's true – has no grandchildren and lives in North Shields. What would you do?"

No answer.

Fergus had had enough.

"It's about him, Betsy, not you. I'm sorry – I've got to go. Due in theatre. Let me know what happens."

Phoebe would never behave like this he thought as he headed off to the staff room for a decent cup of coffee before making his way to the Imaging department.

CHAPTER NINETEEN

"I don't know what's happened to her. She used to be such a nice girl."

Heather Eriksson was sitting at the table in her sterile kitchen. Archie was with her, close, listening attentively to her every word... every syllable. Sometimes he liked to count them. He could see that his mother was not happy but could not understand why. No one had said anything unkind or rude; Siobhan hardly said anything at all, except to his father but that was only when he was awake and taking notice. Most of his time was spent upstairs in bed where he lay in what seemed to be in a doze. He spent hours listening to his iPod through ear phones – Audible or something. Said he was in Barchester going through a lot of Trollope, whatever that meant.

"Is it her clothes?" Perhaps he could help his mother analyse her state of mind. Archie did not like it when she talked like this; it upset equilibrium.

Personally, Archie could not care less what people wore. He liked to be comfortable himself – nothing scratchy or tight. He favoured tracksuits and T shirts; jeans were rough, long sleeved shirts had cuffs and collars that chafed. Siobhan had taken – almost overnight – to wearing nothing but black with occasional slashes of red or purple. Not grungy but stylised, a little bizarre for his taste, awfully scratchy and very tight. Goth she had said it was called when he had found her in her room filling suitably black bin liners with the wardrobe of her youth. She had grown beyond all that crap apparently; it was to go to a charity shop for the less enlightened who were welcome to wear what they wanted ... but Siobhan would not be seen dead in it. This had puzzled Archie. Her obsession with death and its sartorial manifestation appeared to contradict her desire not to appear deceased in what she wore, especially as she seemed to have assumed a state of perpetual mourning and used make up that made her look like a corpse.

Heather's reply was mournful. "Her clothes are certainly part of it. Why does she always look so ... morbid?"

"Angst. From the German, a feeling of deep anxiety or dread, typically an unfocused one about the human condition or the state of the world in general. The word also occurs in Danish, Norwegian and Dutch."

"Really? Fascinating." She meant it. "But why does she feel like this?"

"Her age. It's common in adolescents, especially girls. I expect she'll grow out of it. They all do."

"Darling Archie." Heather reached for his hand which he withdrew and placed carefully on his lap under the table. "Thank goodness for your common sense. I've no idea what she's got to be so worried about. I did wonder if it was your father's health but he's stable and all we have to do is wait for a more suitable liver then he'll be completely well again. ... I feel sorry for whoever was persuaded to take that organ. Thank goodness we won't have to go through something like that. ... D'you think Siobhan's still angry that we refused the marginal one?"

Archie was sanguine. Surely not? It had been an informed and sensible decision based on careful evaluation of the pros and the cons. No, she was just going through a difficult age. According to what he had read on the internet this was a phenomenon among teenage girls. Although he did not agree with it because it was politically incorrect and he knew that it was not socially acceptable to subscribe to such opinions, he could understand why women were labelled hysterical.

At which point Heather decided to change the conversation. Would he like another slice of toast? Lightly browned, crustless, left to cool so that the butter did not run, just the way he liked it?

Ted categorically refused to attend the second appointment with the consultant. He planted his foot firmly on the ground, balanced himself against the back of the armchair and brandished his stump in defiance. He was not going and that was an end of it. Would not even get into the wheelchair in case Betsy got behind the handles and pushed him where he did not want to go. And that went for Lizzie too he said darkly, even though she was not there but just in case Betsy got ideas. The girls had formed an uneasy truce which had, at first, seemed gratifying. All he had ever wanted. Now however, he was regretting their alliance, heartily wishing for them to be at war once more so that he could sit back unnoticed and pursue his own agenda. At least Lizzie could be relied upon to back her father against her sister should it become necessary but, in the end, Betsy had capitulated with extremely bad grace and dire prognostications about what would happen to him. All of which he ignored and drenched in alcohol.

Betsy rang the hospital and got herself put through to the consultant. Initially he was reluctant to talk to her – she was not the patient but when she explained what her father had decided, he was more forthcoming. Yes, she would need to know the results of the scan in order to arrange appropriate care. Which, he was sorry to say, would have to be essentially palliative. Mr Jones had advanced cancer of the colon – stage 3. They could operate but the outcome was uncertain. Any chemotherapy would have to be aggressive and there was no guarantee that the cancer had not already metastasised so, all things considered, the choice her father had made was understandable. Perhaps even right – who was he to say? The hospital could help with organising palliative care; Betsy was a doctor; her father would be in good hands. Ms Jones would be with her father presumably ... until the end? No, she of course knew that no exact timing could be given but, in view of the severity of the cancer, it would not be long. Weeks? Perhaps days if the cancer caused an obstruction. As always with these things it was impossible to say but the prognosis was terminal. No doubt about it. If there was anything the consultant or the hospital could do to help... he was so sorry, but thank you for letting them know and freeing up limited resources for other patients. As one consultant to another, he gave her his mobile number and asked her to keep him informed. He would be happy to talk to her anytime. He wished her good luck.

For the first time Betsy fully realised that her father was going to die. She also realised how the language of the experts resonated with their patients. One of the most ominous things that a patient could hear was a senior clinician wishing them good luck, not as they were leaving hospital after treatment but before it had even started. It was a death sentence. 'You're an interesting case' or 'we don't often see something like this' were guaranteed to raise the blood pressure of any discerning invalid but were not in themselves the end of the world. However, when medics lowered their voices, looked you in the eye and said good luck with much the same solicitude as a priest delivering the last rites, then you knew that you were in big trouble. Betsy heard and understood. The finality, the hopelessness, the 'nothing we can do except make it more comfortable and ease the passing.'

She wept. Ted didn't.

Hugh Goldberg was peering over his glasses.

"It was my understanding that these incidents had been shelved. Dealt with; lessons learned and moved on. You must have good reason to revisit them, Jeremy. At least, I hope you do."

He ostentatiously glanced at his watch and tried not to sigh. As if he did not have enough to do without this. He looked wistfully at his computer screen, clicked save and closed the email he had been writing. It was already overdue and he did not like being rushed, any more than he liked being late. But Jeremy had insisted on seeing him; Debbie had managed to find a non-existent gap in the daily schedule so here he was, and Hugh did not like what he was hearing. None of it.

"Does Phoebe know?"

Jeremy shook his head.

"No, of course not. I wanted to discuss it with you first."

This was not quite true; Jeremy omitted to mention his clandestine conversations with other senior colleagues about his concerns. If pressed he would have argued that he had merely been sounding out his fellow clinicians. What? Him? A personal agenda? Certainly not. Patient safety was of paramount importance; they all shared the same view, didn't they? It was fundamental to the achievement of best practice which in turn led to the successful outcomes that they all sought, well, all but one it seemed. It saddened him to have to acknowledge it, but Professor Dennington – in whom they had all invested such belief and trust – was putting patients at risk. Not deliberately, he was sure (the alternative was unimaginable) but carelessness

– probably. Possibly incompetence but he preferred not to pass judgement, at this stage. Or maybe arrogance he had then added, thoughtfully, as if it had only just occurred to him, at which point he had moved on to other things and left the planted, watered, fertilized seed to germinate and bloom in the fertile ground of the ambitious senior medic in whose ear he had been pouring poison.

"Why now?" Hugh was not so much suspicious as perplexed – an emotion that was becoming unpleasantly familiar.

Jeremy paused, to be seen to consider, then to overtly choose his words with great care. No one would be able to accuse him of slander or gossip.

"It started when Professor Dennington intervened in my procedure recently – the IVC re-section."

He looked at the Medical Director who, yes, knew exactly to what he was referring. How could he not? In addition to the discussion with Phoebe, Debbie had filled him in on the hospital version of the event. He had also learned that Jeremy was known as Jack Ass and that had made him wonder if he had a nickname, but Debbie would not be drawn on that one. Jeremy was still talking though, measured, deliberate and thoughtfully. The man seemed genuinely concerned as he clasped his hands in distress, hanging onto his fingers for comfort. Hugh peered over his glasses to listen more closely. Anything to do with patient safety had to be taken seriously – extremely seriously. Jeremy began to reference notes from what now Hugh saw was an extremely hefty ring binder file in which all 'the cases' were apparently stored. JA was prepared; the most pertinent pages were marked with post it notes, his arsenal of evidence loaded, ready and waiting to refer to all those occasions when Phoebe had been remiss. Hugh could not avoid the possibility that she was indeed a problem. A threat? It would have to be investigated. Jeremy had been right to insist on seeing him. The email would have to wait.

JA wondered if this was how it felt to be high as he strode purposefully away from Hugh's office. The secretary – what was her name? – had looked surprised when he had thanked her for fitting him in at such short notice. Perhaps she was not always so efficient, although it was more likely that as most people did not have his good manners, an expression of gratitude had astonished her. The demise in social graces was so regrettable; thank heavens he had been to a decent university and knew how to conduct himself. It was there that he had learned to make a point of acknowledging those who might be of some use in the future. Talking of which, there was that jobbing anaesthetist coming down the corridor towards him - the one who had helped out Betsy Jones when Dennington had usurped him in theatre. Fergus something...

"Fergus! How are you?" JA was all affability and handshakes. Fergus stopped – it was impossible not to and waited, with interest. He had never so much as been acknowledged by JA before, not that he cared, but this was an interesting development and he was curious about this sudden change of behaviour. It was certainly nothing to do with friendship, of that he was certain. The image of Vikki with her bottle blonde hair loose on her naked shoulders floated into his mind and he smiled. JA smiled back. Did Fergus have a moment for a quick chat? – JA knew how busy he was but yes, it was important. He would like to run something past Fergus; pick his brains; it would not take a minute but he felt it was of particular relevance to such a senior anaesthetist. Fergus continued to smile, more broadly as he mentally undressed Vikki and recalled the singular row of moles on her bikini line as JA approached closer, all the better to be more confidential. It was necessary to be discreet he said; what he had to say was of a sensitive nature and open to misinterpretation if it reached the wrong ears. However, he knew that Fergus was a professional, a man of integrity and understood that everything JA was about to say was based on the most ethical of principles. Nothing was more important than patient safety.

Fergus listened as JA murmured. He no longer smiled. This was Phoebe that the man was maligning. And he was definitely maligning her. Had JA forgotten that Fergus had been there when Phoebe had taken over during the debacle in theatre 4 and prevented a potential catastrophe? Or perhaps he assumed, as so many bloody surgeons did, that anaesthetists saw and heard nothing? That they just sat there at the top of the body, feeding in the oxygen and the drugs, paid extras while the starring roles danced and pivoted with their scalpels and their egos over the rest of the body lying before them. All the table a stage and they the players.

And he was glad that he had slept with JA's wife. It had been meant as a one off, a quickie to prove a point but now, how easy it was to decide that he would do it again. It was also equally easy to resolve to tell Betsy what JA was saying before he got to her himself. However, it did not take an Oxford PhD to work out that if JA had taken the trouble to tell a bit-player like Fergus, he must already have spoken to other more central characters. To JA he said not a word in reply, merely raised an eyebrow and looked over the man's shoulder as if to ascertain that they were not being overheard. Jeremy took this as tacit agreement: co-conspirators, mum's the word, another convert to the cause. For Fergus, the only dilemma was wondering whether or not to tell Phoebe. He would have to think about that but whatever happened, something had to be done.

The receptionist in Imaging was annoyed. The department was

busy, there was a queue of patients still to be processed and it was time for her lunch break. Which She Was Entitled To. Didn't she have rights and needs, just like everyone else? Not only had she had been trying, in vain, to get hold of Vikki Albright about a particularly obnoxious and persistent patient who was determined not to wait but her fellow receptionist had also disappeared. Well, it was her lunch hour. She was going to take it.

Grabbing her handbag she levered herself out of her chair and abandoned post – swiftly, so that she was out of range when the queue became irate. Not her problem. Not for the moment anyway, and just to make sure she resolved to find a quiet corner in which to consume her pasty, crisps, Scotch egg, grapes and energy drink. God knows, she needed the sustenance. People simply did not understand how much stress and pressure was involved in being an NHS receptionist on the frontline in a busy department – and Imaging was always busy. Why, if she had known herself, she'd never have taken the job and even now was only doing it until something better came along.

Ah, that would do. The linen cupboard. Out of the way, discreet, windowless with a shelf of stationery if anyone found her. Perfect. She had to push the door hard to open it; there seemed to be something wedged behind. Really, people were so careless: simply threw the piles of clean linen on the shelves; it was no wonder they fell onto the floor, which was always grubby but at least that meant she would have something to sit on while she ate her lunch.

The door refused to budge. She put down her handbag, inhaled deeply, stepped back then hurled her substantially-Over-BMI frame against the door, shoulder first. It shivered, held for a moment, then pitched itself inwards. Inside, the light was on which was a surprise, but not half as much as the sight of Dr Crombie standing upright before her without his trousers. Crouched before him, on her knees, was Vikki Albright. The shiny blonde hair on the back of her head quivered in the artificial light. Her face was buried in his groin. He was gripping her head with both hands, clinging onto her hair like the handlebars of a bike in danger of going out of control.

"Come in" he said. "Plenty of room for one more."

CHAPTER TWENTY

Siobhan, the once nice girl was now a very angry one. She had received an invitation via Snapchat to a party and her mother was to blame. It was all Heather's fault.

"I'm going out on Saturday" she had announced, defiant, battle ready.

They were in the kitchen, all of them except Graham who was, as always, resting upstairs. He was permanently exhausted these days, partly due to the medication he took to quell the itching that plagued him all his waking life not to mention the discomfort of the ascites that wore his body like a water-filled balloon. Mother and son were sitting at the kitchen table in their usual places, opposite each other so that they could more easily chat and share confidences. Siobhan had materialised unseen in the doorway, dark, moody, brooding. The spectre at the feast.

Heather was taken unawares which pleased her daughter enormously. It was exactly what she had intended; a surprise assault when the enemy was resting, disarmed, in camp. Archie was there – when was he not? – but Siobhan had already discounted any contribution he might make. Moral and verbal support such as his were nothing she could not deal with. She focussed on her mother, who had retaliated.

"I don't know anything about this... Where?"

"A party."

There was a stunned silence. Archie gaped. A party? Was his sister mad? Why would anyone want to go to a party, especially dressed like that? She was too young, his mother would not allow it, how would she get there ... and back again? It would be late. She might drink alcohol or do drugs. What was the matter with her? He studied his mother with the same intensity as his sister to see how she would react.

"I beg your pardon?"

So, her mother was going to play the astonished, disappointed, perplexed where did I go wrong card? Siobhan tried not to smile in triumph. This was all going according to meticulous plan, mused and mulled over most of the night in the privacy of her bedroom which she was also planning to paint black, but she would save that for later.

"You heard."

Heather gasped. Archie gaped anew. He looked like some sort of short haired pimply goldfish struggling to breathe outside a bowl; in a second or two he would start flapping his hands. Siobhan pursued her advantage, bearing down on them from higher ground as she stood and they sat.

"It's a special party ... A celebration of life.... Something I knew you would approve of."

This was completely unexpected – unprecedented, and Heather was caught off guard. Where was this going? Who was this girl? What had happened to her daughter?

"Well, yes, but whose party is it?"

"A lad at school. Someone in my year who you don't know. But..." she paused. Poised. "Someone whose mother has just had a successful liver transplant which is great, but this is even better because the liver was marginal and had been rejected by someone else ... but it works perfectly and his mother – step mother actually – has made a full recovery and now she can lead a normal life."

Dramatic pause. Let it sink in. Suck that up, mother.

"So, they're celebrating. Having a party. And I'm going."

"Am I invited?"

Now it was the turn of Siobhan and Heather to gape, to stare at Archie, bonded by mutual wonder.

"It sounds like a good idea. I'd like to go too."

Poor Siobhan; this was so outside any anticipated development in any direction of the conversation that she had planned that she was utterly floored. However, Heather now found herself, by the strangest of means, somehow on trial. She had heard what Siobhan had said – every loaded word - and was mortified with guilt and fear. Graham must never know. They had made the right decision; they had. It must be circumstantial. What worked for one would not work for another. Graham was a special case; they could not take the risk. This other woman must have been desperate or not so ill or a better physical match or something else, perhaps a different blood type or her illness had been different to Graham's so made her less of a risk. It was good that the woman had survived and got better, but that didn't mean that it would have worked for Graham. ... Would it?

Heather studied her children. One, dressed in black, eyes like crows against chalk, the other in a saggy tracksuit beneath the face of an earnest cub scout contemplating a camping trip. The younger, who seemed so old, world weary, defined by fury and bitterness and the older, so young, so innocent, so pure. Had she done this? She pulled herself together.

"Neither of you is going and that's an end of it. I'm glad for this other family that their transplant has been a success but it has nothing to do with us. It's a completely different set of circumstances and I'm surprised at you Siobhan, for being so insensitive." Her turn now to pause, disarm her opponent, regroup and strike back.

"How would your father feel if he heard about this? What would it do to him? After all his recent disappointment? He must never hear of it. It would kill him."

Siobhan the murderess, Heather in triumph, Archie none the wiser.

Graham continued to doze upstairs in bed, completely out of it.

Amber was out of bed – all the time except when obliged to return to it at night in time for the hospital lights out. Her medication was frequent and substantial but already becoming part of her daily (Jah be praised) life. She would return to base on the ward for the arrival of the drugs trolley, restrain herself enough to sit down either on her bed or beside it and dutifully down the cocktail presented by the presiding staff nurse. Then she would be off to create more noise, distraction and disturbance. When could she go home? Wouldn't they be glad to see the back of her? (They would). She had a party to plan. Everyone was invited without exception – everyone – especially Professor Dennington. Agwe could not bring himself to call her Phoebe as Amber did. The two women had become surprisingly relaxed with each other. For Amber it was easy; she loved everybody and it was hard not to want to like her. The Ice Queen had been hard to thaw but as it had never occurred to Amber that they would be anything but friends, Phoebe was disarmed and prone to temporary bouts of excessive melting when they met. Instant refreezing however took place as soon as they parted company so no harm done.

"You will come, won't you?" Amber was entreating during the final ward round. So much for her exit interview – Phoebe had not been able to get in a word. "It's on Saturday – starts in the afternoon and goes on until it ends, whenever that is. But you can come any time – in the morning if it's easier. Please come, Phoebe. We owe you so much. It wouldn't be the same if you didn't."

Agwe's mane was being heartily shaken in agreement. They would be honoured if she'd come; there were so many people wanted to meet her and say thank you. It was just such a shame that they couldn't invite the donor's family. Yes, they'd sent a letter which Ann (also invited and who had said she might drop by) had forwarded but no, they hadn't heard anything. But hey, early days! They lived in hope. All their family and friends would be there. (They did not yet know that Agwe's son had not only issued an open invitation on Snapchat but had now also included Facebook). It was going to be massive (it was indeed) but they didn't care. Life was for living. There would be lots of Rastas yeah, but she needn't worry about being a transplant surgeon and that. She had restored Amber back to health and that was all that mattered. Live and let live, yeah?

Phoebe was touched, but not sufficiently to unequivocally accept the invitation. She told them she was delighted, of course, to be invited but could not promise: her schedule was so unpredictable. She would do her best to attend but if another transplant or some kind of emergency came up, she knew they would understand that it had to take priority. It was also very kind of them to include anyone else she might want to bring with her but no, there wasn't anybody. If she came, she would come alone. This was listened to with great interest by her ward round retinue. The Ice Queen's private life was something of a hospital mystery and the source of much speculation as Phoebe well knew - and was extremely careful to cultivate.

Whatever happened, she and Amber would meet in clinic for follow ups – probably Agwe too? Vigorous head and mane activity assured her that they would. Phoebe had no qualms about having already resolved to be unavoidably detained at the time of the party and therefore, most regrettably, unable to attend, but she did not want to hurt anyone's feelings. Cold yes, but not yet callous. How could she do her job if she did not care?

Fergus was in unexpected discomfort. His anger with Jeremy Albright was almost exceeded by his indignation on behalf of Phoebe whom, he had begun to realise, he really quite liked. He enjoyed being in her company even when they did not have sex. Perhaps he was getting old. His fling with Vikki was already tedious and since the unfortunate encounter with the fat receptionist from Imaging in the linen cupboard, was very public knowledge. He could only hope that JA had heard about it. But now that he had breached JA, as it were, there was nothing left to interest him, not even the discovery of moles in secret places. He did have confirmation though, that blonde was not her natural hair colour.

Ted was dying. It had set in with constipation that at first was uncomfortable and then became a monster. Everything was stuck he told Betsy. He couldn't even fart anymore for feck's sake. Lizzie and Betsy had settled on an uneasy tacit truce and were often in the flat together, moving so self-consciously around each other that Ted wanted to slap them. But that was before his abdomen became distended; bigger by the day, hard, stretched, solid. He no longer sat in the wheelchair or even the armchair – he could not bend – but lay on his bed, a granite hummock under striped flannel sheets, blanket, eiderdown and a candlewick bedspread. The girls had both, independently, suggested that a duvet might be more comfortable – lighter over his increasing mound – but Ted had given them short shrift.

"It's too fecking late for me to start changing my bed clothes" he said. "I've had sheets and blankets all me life. What was good enough then, 's good enough now. They'll see me out. ... It won't be long.... I 'll have another wet though." At which point he had nodded to the empty whisky glass on the bedside table. "And don't look at me like that..." he had reprimanded Lizzie.

"Should he be drinking this much?" she had asked Betsy. "It can't be good for him."

"I don't think it matters."

"What happens next?"

"He's got an obstruction which is why he's so swollen. The colon will eventually perforate and he'll get sepsis but by that time he'll probably have lost consciousness, his blood pressure will drop and then it's only a matter of time. ... Sorry. But you did ask."

"When?"

"Not long. A few days? Maybe less ... He knows."

"I don't think he cares."

He didn't. However, there were a couple of things that Ted wanted sorted out before he shuffled off, he said.

"I want a proper burial. Catholic. A Requiem Mass, the works. And when I'm six feet under you can do what you like, but no black and no mourning.... And I want the last rites when the time comes."

"But Dad, you're lapsed." Betsy was appalled.

Ted took a deep draught from his glass, drained it and handed it to Lizzie for refilling. Betsy was so like her mother he thought, judgemental. No wonder she wasn't married.

"The priest knows. I've already told him.... It's always there, y'know."

"Father Achill?" Lizzie said, still holding the almost empty pub size bottle of whisky with the upside-down labels.

"The church?" Betsy asked at the same time.

"Aidan, aye that's the fella" Ted answered daughter number two then, to his firstborn said, "Yes. Saw me in so it'll see me out. And not a wake afterwards but a party; a bloody good one. A proper send off. In the pub. You're to drink to me and then get on with life, d'you hear me? I'll fecking haunt you if you don't."

"He would too" Betsy said to Lizzie when they had poured him another drink and he had dozed off in his bedroom while the two women sat together in front of the fake fire and drank tea. "I hate that bloody fire."

"At least we agree on something... Thanks for not putting sugar in my tea."

Betsy smiled before she began to cry.

At the Midland Central, Phoebe was beginning to feel uncertain. Whenever she arrived somewhere, people seemed to leave. It was not immediate or a mass exodus but a more gradual dissemination, a general emptiness that prevailed after she had been in a room or even a corridor for more than a few minutes. The corridors were long and places for moving on but even so, there had always been people there, walking past, speaking, stopping for a comment or a brief chat, sometimes huddles of miscellaneous medics. Hidden in plain sight, it was an ideal place to 'bump' into someone or exchange news and gossip, the subterranean life blood of the hospital. The staff room was the same, not that she went there often but when she did present herself as decorum required for a decent cup of coffee and a social interaction with her colleagues, the room would quietly empty. A few words, a general greeting and then she found it was just her and the coffee machine. It was perplexing. And unsettling. She had no idea why it was this way. At first it had seemed unimportant, coincidental. Hospitals were such busy places and everyone had to be somewhere else but when it persisted, she could not help but notice. Fergus alone seemed immune to the disease. In fact, she seemed to see a great deal of him. Obviously he was covering for Betsy Jones who had some sort of family crisis to attend to, so they worked together in theatre much more frequently at the moment but why was it he was always there, when everyone else was not? There was no intimacy at work; absolutely out of the question she had told him from the very first, with no exceptions. Ever. And he had adhered to the injunction, which was gratifying if not a little unexpected, so their relationship (if you could call it that) had continued longer than she had anticipated. Had she said something? Done something? Senior colleagues could be so sensitive. They had such big egos but such fragile self-esteem that the slightest hint of criticism or innuendo might send them into a maelstrom of diva-like proportions. Not her of course, she never took any notice of such nonsense, except that all this 'not quite being ignored' but 'definitely being avoided' was unsettling. It was beginning to bother even her.

Fergus too, had noticed. He rang Betsy.

She was delighted to hear from him even though her news was bad. The worst.

"He's dying" she said when the lover enquired about the father. "It won't be long, thank God, for his sake. But if the cancer doesn't get him the whisky will."

"Sounds like my kind of man" Fergus commented, mind elsewhere. "Betsy, there's something I want to discuss with you, that we need to talk about as soon as possible."

Here it comes she thought. At last. Absence really does make the heart grow fonder. Oh, it would be lovely to be able to tell Dad that I'm getting married or at least in a permanent relationship before he dies. Yes. Yes. Yes.

"It's about Phoebe."

"Professor Dennington?"

"Yes. JA is up to something." He proceeded to outline, in some detail, what JA had said to him and presumably everybody else judging by their behaviour. How long did Betsy think her father had to go? Because as soon as she got back to work, he felt that she and he should go to Hugh Goldberg and put the record straight about what happened in theatre 4 – the IVC resection – she remembered, didn't she? He'd come in to help her put in a line? Oh yes, she remembered, very well. How could she forget how close he had stood to her, the sexual frisson, the hot wetness between her legs?

"I think so" she said. "When Dennington took over from JA?"

"Phoebe. Yes."

Pause. Silence.

"Betsy?" Yes, she was still there. "I'm sorry about your father. Are you okay?"

No, she wasn't, but she wasn't going to tell him that. She would let him know, yes, when the delirium pallor began so that they would have a clearer idea of just how long Ted had left. Just a few hours probably, once perforation and sepsis set in. But then there would be the funeral to sort out ... and everything else ... it would be at least a week, probably 2, maybe 3 before she could even think of getting back to work. Could Phoebe wait that long?

She felt sick when she ended the call. Lizzie was out, so she went into the kitchen to look for something to eat.

CHAPTER TWENTY-ONE

Norma had decided that it was time to stop floating. The little bird was going to clip her wings. It was nothing to do with getting on with life or getting over her loss but perhaps something to do with coming to terms with it. Alan was always there. But she sensed that he was getting annoyed with her; indecision had always frustrated him. Got to get on with things pet, he had said and she could hear him now. That was why she now found herself outside the charity shop in the precinct. Not the big one with all the fancy window displays but the one further up the road, slightly out of the way, quieter and run by an older woman, not one of those smart young lasses she had watched wasping around the others. She studied the notice in the window – handwritten which made her feel less intimidated – asking for volunteers and wondered if anyone inside had noticed how many times she had stood there reading it.

"Go on pet, you can do it" she heard Alan say, so she opened the door and went in.

Well past fifty, almost as short as she was but thrice as round, the manageress who said she was always just called Maz greeted Norma with such enthusiasm that she found she did not want 'to think about it' but would be happy to help out 'now and then' when they were short staffed. Was she busy today? Perhaps she'd like to stay for a coffee – or tea - and see how they did things, not that there was much to see? Maz was on her own - nothing more short staffed than that - would love the company; they could sit at the till with a cup of tea and Norma could meet the customers. Lots of them were regulars and came in for the company. Did Norma know anything about knitting? She did! Wonderful! They had been given a sizeable donation of wool, needles and patterns which needed sorting and Maz did not know one end of a needle from the other. The pricing was easy and Norma would soon get the hang of the price gun thingie. How did she like her tea? No sugar! Well, wasn't she good? Maz was trying to give it up; Norma could help her and they were going to get on just champion.

As she sat and drank tea, watching the occasional customers on the shop floor and listening to Maz chat to her, to them, to anyone who would listen, Norma felt for the first time since his death that although Alan was still beside her, he had stood back – just a few steps. She was still tethered to him but the chair she sat on felt solid. The wool in her hands was soft, the steel needles were cold and she heard their high-pitched chatter as they rubbed and quarrelled with each other in their cardboard box. Only when they were separated and paired by size did they quieten and settle which made Norma feel calm and useful. Useful. It felt good. She began to sift through the patterns with interest, organising them first into child and adult then becoming more ambitious, grouping them according to gender and then, into design type. Maz was thrilled. When Norma finally went home and opened the front door she was not alone. Alan was there, of course, but so too were Maz's praises.

"You're a natural, Norma pet. Are you sure you've never done this before? Well, this is a lucky day for me. Will I see you tomorrow?"

So, when the phone rang Norma could honestly say as she answered that she was that sorry if she sounded breathless but she had just come in after a busy morning ... sorry, who was it? Rosni? Rosni Chatterjee, the organ donation lady? ... What? ... A letter? From the recipient? Oh yes, yes please. She did want it. Very much.

"Alan. Did you hear that?" she said as she put the receiver back into the cradle. "We've got a letter from the person who's got your liver. Rosni's going to forward it to us."

"You're a doctor. Why can't you do something? He's in agony."

Lizzie had turned from the Macmillan nurse who had shaken her head by way of an apologetic refusal and was accosting Betsy. Ted lay between them, moaning. His eyes were closed but his face thrashed, his hands clenched into themselves and his thin leg was pulled up towards his swollen belly; the stump lay rigid and useless. He might have been giving birth except that his cargo was poison, eating him alive, with nowhere else to go. He was being devoured.

"There must be something you can give him!"

Betsy and the nurse exchanged glances. Nothing was said – it did not need to be. He's had the maximum dose; I can't give him any more. I'd lose my registration the nurse's eyes said. It'd be murder.

"He's had as much as he's allowed, Lizzie. He can't have any more, not yet."

"But he needs it. Look!"

He did. A spasm of pain had twisted Ted's eyes into knots, tied up with the contortions of his face. His mouth was a formless line, strung between hollow cheeks sagging away from the thin ridge of his nose; a shrivelled landscape, shifting and changing in time to the rhythm of his agony.

"Why can't you give him more? It's not going to make any difference at this stage and it'll stop his suffering. It's awful. What's the matter with you?"

Lizzie was shouting now, mostly at her sister but the nurse was included for good measure. The latter said nothing. Grief manifested itself in many forms and she had learned that it was better to remain quiet and let relatives rant. She reckoned that the patient would soon be so out of it that the pain would no longer be an issue but this was an interesting case. She was intrigued to see how the consultant daughter would cope with the situation. Apparently, she was an anaesthetist in a trauma unit, one of those centres of excellence, where people died all the time. But to look at her you would never know it. She seemed a complete mess – all rheumy eyed and dishevelled, like she hadn't slept in weeks and needed a good bath. Certainly a hair wash. The other one, the half-sister, was much more together even though she was the one who was shouting.

"I know she's not allowed to dole out the morphine but you're a doctor, Betsy. Why don't you do something?"

"I can't, Lizzie. I'm not allowed. Not since Shipman."

"Shipman? But this is completely different. He was just a crazy GP. We're not trying to kill Dad, just put a stop to his suffering. It'd be different if he was in hospital – you'd let him have whatever he needed if he was in hospital, everyone knows that."

Betsy did not want to argue, not even with Lizzie. Besides, she had a point. Time was - before Shipman - when the dose of morphine for hospital patients such as Ted would simply be doubled every day until their suffering really did come to an end. Minimal pain for the patient; less suffering for everyone. No one committing murder.

"It's different now, Lizzie. I can't prescribe any more in case it shortens his life."

"Christ! Betsy! Listen to yourself. He's dying. In agony. And you're worried about shortening his life. What's the matter with you people?"

Now Lizzie was talking to both doctor and nurse. "Give me the morphine and I'll administer it. Leave the room or something, I don't care. Say I forced you to it. It's my responsibility – I don't care what happens to me. Dad can't go on like this."

Betsy was crying, again. She couldn't think of anything else to do.

"Perhaps..." it was the MacMillan nurse. Treading warily. "You could contact your father's GP – discuss it with him. He might be able to increase the dose..."

"Yes!" Betsy, clutching at straws, wiping snot from her nose up her face into her hair.

Lizzie stared.

"D'you think he will?"

"I have no fucking idea. But I'm calling him. Now." Betsy was already transferring snot from her fingers onto her mobile phone.

"I need to speak to him immediately. I am a consultant anaesthetist from Midland Central and this is urgent. Put me through, please. Time is of the essence." God, I sound like Phoebe Dennington, Betsy rued as she waited. Clearly the female receptionist at the other end of the phone was weakening. Doctors she knew only too well and took no notice – had worked in local practice long enough not to take them seriously – but a consultant... from an out of area city hospital. Such a consultant was one up on any GP and even the clinicians from the local hospital, most of whom she knew by name anyway.

I wonder what it's about she thought as she told Jim Lerwick who was on the phone. Lerwick was a networker but ... Midland Central? Jim had much the same thought as he took the call.

"Dr James Lerwick" he announced as Betsy came on the line.

"Damn" he thought as she identified herself. "I should have known." Nevertheless, he listened to her with a fixed face.

"No. I can't do that. I'm sorry but he's on the maximum I feel comfortable in prescribing at the moment. I understand that he's in discomfort and how distressing it is, especially for you and your sister, but it's impossible to increase the dosage. I'm sure you understand that better than anyone, as a consultant anaesthetist." He hoped he sounded sympathetic. "We don't have enough syringe drivers available otherwise I could get him one of those... Do you want me to try and get him into a hospice? I know that there's a few days wait and he might not make it that long, but I could try ..."

The patient in his consulting room was listening intently and would no doubt relay the entire conversation with glorious embellishment throughout the entire practice area and beyond, hopefully in Lerwick's favour. No one wanted to be called Shipman but no one wanted to be classed as callous either.

"I'm in the middle of a consultation ... "

Sorry he mouthed at the patient who indicated that she was more than happy for him to continue. This was so much more entertaining than haemorrhoids. If only she knew who he was talking about. Maybe the receptionist would tell her.

Betsy rang off.

"Bastard" she shouted at the snotty phone. Neither Lizzie nor the nurse took any notice. Ted was still writhing but had stopped moaning – it was just too much effort. When would it end?

"Perhaps this might be a good time to call the priest." It was the nurse again, less wary. Someone had to take control.

"The priest! Oh God! I'd forgotten... Lizzie?"

"It's all arranged. He's on stand-by. All I have to do is call – he's just down the road. No, I'll use mine thanks." Lizzie reached for her own phone in her handbag and left the room.

Betsy resumed her crying.

Father Achill – a good looking young man who ran marathons and did not eat meat breezed into the bedroom as if stopping at a watering station en route to a finish line. He had jogged up from the vestry he said - surprisingly little traffic - and here he was; how are you Ted? Ah. Let's get on with it shall we?

The nurse left the room, mostly because space was so limited. Lizzie stood on one side of the bed, opposite the priest while Betsy stood at the end of it and watched, a tear-stained adjudicator. To her astonishment her father stopped writhing, laid down his leg beside the stump and lay quietly in front of them; eyes still closed, hands fiercely clenched but face a little smoother than it had been. There was no other reaction to what the priest said and did, not a sound, not a movement, even when he was touched, but it was obvious that something was happening and that Ted was aware of it. Somewhere, in his world, where they could not go, he was still with them.

Lizzie and Aidan Achill seemed to know each other well. Betsy was annoyed. Since when had her sister been religious? She wasn't a church goer but that didn't seem to matter from the way they were talking; it was all about community apparently judging by their conversation: a community in which Betsy had no part. She had been introduced to the priest of course. No, not Father Achill - just Aidan, please he begged – preferred to keep things personal and informal he said. God didn't need titles. Ted was a lovely man and it'd been a privilege to know him. They'd had long chats about his childhood and the role of the Irish Catholic church which, thankfully, was so different now.

The reasoning behind Ted's decision to – temporarily - reject his faith was illuminating and had helped Aidan define his own sense of vocation. No man should be forced into the priesthood; Ted had been right to refuse.

"Dad was going to be a priest?" Betsy was incredulous. "But he hates the church. And he's not dead yet so don't talk about him in the past tense".

Aidan smiled, touched her on the arm and accompanied Lizzie out of the room. Betsy smouldered.

Ted was going out with the light. Now he was motionless, somewhere else. Lizzie and Betsy sat beside him, on either side of the ancient candlewick bedspread. His thin body barely interrupted the balding, once proud, vibrant pattern. Now, like Ted, it lay motionless and pallid. Only his belly protruded up under the bedclothes, a soft pink drumlin, dominating the otherwise featureless landscape which draped and fell away from him with the departing day.

"Did you know about Dad and this priesthood thing, Lizzie?"

Yes, she did. Only recently though. They'd talked about it after she'd been in touch with Aidan. Dad liked Aidan. Said there was no fecking bullshit about him.

"But what's it about? Why was he going to be a priest?"

"His mother wanted it. He was the eldest son so she dedicated him to the church. Had it all arranged - sent him off to a seminary as soon as he was old enough but he ran away, to England."

"Then what?"

"He got someone pregnant so married her."

Yes, your mother her face said, without movement or emotion.

Betsy was wondering how much else she did not know when Lizzie broke the silence.

"I've never seen anyone die before..."

Was Lizzie looking to her for comfort?

"It's not too bad. Not when it's expected. But this would never have happened if he'd done the right thing and had treatment - and he wouldn't have suffered like this. There was no need for any of this. I don't understand it; he had everything to live for."

The room held its breath as Lizzie stared at Betsy.

"Are you for real? His life was shit."

Now it was Betsy's turn to stare.

"Look around you. Look at this room, this flat. His wheelchair.... His legs. Where could he go? What could he do? Who did he see? Not you that's for sure, down in Birmingham being the great I am."

"You're no better. How often did you see him?"

"Every week."

This was true – just - but the visits had been short and pithy and Lizzie knew it. However, her guilt was nothing to what Betsy ought to feel and she was going to make sure that she did until it became part of her DNA.

"This flat's okay."

"It's crap. Would you live here?"

They both examined the low ceilings, exhausted carpet, paintwork mellowing with nicotine from previous incumbents, the jaundiced nets hanging themselves across the windows, dangling but never falling quite far enough to end their misery. The curtains were not closed – there seemed no point. Unlined sparse cotton coverings, patterned with sprigs of desiccated spring flowers as sprightly as those on a compost heap in a graveyard, did little to keep out the light or the dark. Ted's bedroom seemed to exist in its own dim underpowered lightbulb world in which his bedspread shed the only colour. It felt as if the flat was fading out with its owner.

"He loved my mum."

"He did not. It was a mercy when she died and he could marry mine. They'd been having a thing for ages anyway. If he hadn't been a Catholic, they'd've divorced years ago ... or you'd've been aborted."

If Ted had not suddenly gasped it was not clear what might have happened. Fortunately, he appeared still to be unconscious. Both women were distracted by his open mouth, vertical and hollow in his cheeks, reaching up to his nostrils for air. His lips were moist, shivering, fish gills out of water. He breathed in, long and deep, filling his lungs as if to swim underwater then shut his mouth and let his face collapse into the pillow. Only his nose seemed to exist, pointing heavenwards like a forlorn sign-post sticking out of a snow laden landscape.

"Not long now" Betsy said, hoping to distress her sister. Damn! Didn't she have any feelings?

They both waited. And waited. For an eternity before Ted took another deep, gasping breath. All the air went in and nothing came out and yet, he never seemed to fill or inflate. It was as if he was leaking somewhere: punctured, unable to stop himself from going down.

They waited a long time, both watching his face which never moved, listening for the next gasp. It never came. Instead, his face tried to do it for him. It became clammy as if leaking used up air, waxy and even more pale. His eyes were shut but Betsy knew what she would find if she lifted up an eyelid – a movement now beyond Ted who had left such things for other people to take care of.

She began to weep, noisily. It was then that Lizzie knew her father was dead.

It wasn't the doctor who examined the sightless eyes that had become dull and glazed, like cooked egg white but the shop manageress. It was she who rang the GP, the undertaker, Aidan and the warden of the sheltered accommodation to whom she would speak personally the following morning to discuss vacating the flat. It was she who decided what Ted would wear to his funeral but what about the 'and after'? Hadn't Dad given Betsy specific instructions about that? That's what he'd said to her before the illness really took hold –

"Betsy knows all about it."

So, what were they? Betsy?

"Betsy! Pull yourself together. What did Dad want for after the funeral?"

Betsy did not answer but carried on crying.

At first Fergus could hardly make out what Betsy was saying. He only knew it was her because of the alert that had come up on his screen when the call came through.

"Sorry Phoebe, I've got to take this" he said as he left her office where she was writing up a report about the surgical procedure she had just completed. It had been lengthy and complicated – nothing JA would even attempt. An extended right hemi hepatectomy with extra hepatic biliary resection and lymph node clearance for a cholangiocarcinoma; reconstructed with a Roux loop to the ducts to segments 2 and 3. In other words, chopping out three quarters of a liver, creating the risk of eventual liver failure if improperly executed - assuming that the immediate problem of bleeding to death on the table was overcome. Although she thawed a little, Phoebe never broke sweat, raised her voice or even an eyebrow. She just got on with it. No music – not her style; she preferred to listen to her fingers and set her own rhythm which was picked up by her team who followed, chord for chord.

Fergus loved to watch her. She was so... soothing. Calm. He had no idea how she did it but did know that all those of her colleagues who were now taking her name in vain should witness how she operated, day in, day out. Cold, calculating icy Phoebe; so disliked and distant; a surgical machine with whom all the most capable and ambitious wannabe surgeons wanted to work. No wonder JA felt threatened.

He had stood in as anaesthetist for the same Betsy who was now snivelling incoherently at the end of his phone, somewhere very distant or very deep, possibly underwater, gargling with her air supply.

"What's the matter? I can hardly hear you. ... Oh. I'm sorry ... That was quick .... Probably for the best."

Now he could hear Betsy clearly, every word. So could everyone else. He moved out of the corridor in which he was standing and sought refuge in an empty consulting room, shutting the door behind him in an attempt to contain the tempest. Then, abruptly, it ended.

"Betsy?"

Nothing. Just Fergus and his phone staring at each other in the consulting room. Damn. He had wanted to talk to her about going to see Hugh Goldberg on her return; they needed to put the record straight about Phoebe. He took advantage of the moment to bring up his call history. Damn again. Five missed calls from Vikki Albright. Thank God he had kept his phone on silent. The woman would not leave him alone. He deleted the calls and put her number on block; some people never took the hint.

As he re-emerged into the corridor, he found himself face to chest with that delectable FY1, the one that was so well upholstered. Still all buttoned up to the neck unfortunately but nevertheless he had an excellent idea what lay beneath and he felt cheered. Betsy was so bloody complicated; Vikki had become a drag. Phoebe seemed to so unattainable but was always there so, why not? He moved in a little closer and smiled.

CHAPTER TWENTY-TWO

The shop was warm and bright, noisy enough to be distracting and comforting at the same time. Norma found she was in there more and more, sometimes three or four days a week and always on a Saturday. It broke up the weekend so she had only Sunday to get through which was manageable. When she had cleaned and sorted out the laundry – such as there was, she would head over to Alan's grave site for a bit chat and company. There was no headstone as yet but she had it planned. They had discussed it and once the plot had settled, in about a year, then she would have a lovely marble headstone engraved with Alan's name and dates put up. No expense spared pet, but nothing tacky or showy. She knew that wasn't what he wanted. Not for nothing had she sat beside him that many times talking over what he wanted her to do. She had also told him all about Maz and the shop, the customers who came in, what they bought, the donations people made, the amount of money they took and what it would be used for. He knew what she had for her lunch when she was working, how Maz liked her tea ever so sweet and hadn't cut down on sugar or lost weight, not an ounce; even what she watched on the telly. It was champion that his little bird was getting out and about; he was that proud of her. Always with her, she knew that, but she had to learn to fly by herself now. He knew she'd choose the right headstone, just the way they'd agreed. It didn't matter that he was there and she wasn't, they could still chat just the way they always did. Comfortable and cosy, just like in their front room or over the kitchen table. Champion.

The young woman could only open the door by pushing her back against it, armed with the weight of the two black sacks. It worked. The unexpected onslaught caught the door by surprise and it flung itself aside, anxious to assist. Likewise, Norma, who left the safety of behind the counter and pattered out across the shop floor to hold the door open. It looked like a sizeable donation. The young woman beneath it was slender and looked dishevelled. Moving house? A broken relationship that she was clearing out? So many people split up after the Christmas holidays apparently; Maz had told her all about it. They left their past in old suitcases and bin liners for the volunteers to sort out in the cluttered room beyond the shop floor: strangers sifting out the profit and loss of other people's lives. The saddest donations came from those who had died. Worthless treasures from walls and mantelpieces, dusted and loved then discarded by those who came after who neither knew nor understood. A lifetime consigned to a bargain or recycling.

The young woman staggered her way across the floor to the counter and dumped her load beside it with obvious relief. She was sweating, wore no make up and spoke with only an edge of a local accent.

"It's mostly men's clothes" she announced as she straightened herself back into human form. "In quite good condition but a bit dated I'm afraid."

"No bother, pet. We take all sorts" Norma replied. There was something familiar about the lass but she had no idea what. Perhaps she had been in before.

"D'you do Gift Aid?" she asked. If the lass was a regular she would, but then again, perhaps she had only come in to a bit shopping. They had lots of younger customers, all looking for vintage stuff as well as the slightly older ones who had watched that Antiques Roadshow programme on the telly and were on the lookout for a fortune. Maz was well upsides with those ones – she always watched all them antique programmes and knew how to use the internet whadyoucallit thingie where you could find out what everything was worth. Anything promising was put in the glass-fronted bookcase in the back for appraisal by the local auctioneer who liked to pop in for a cup of tea on Wednesdays, the day before viewings day. Not that there was ever much to appraise. But still the fortune seekers came and bought, oh, all sorts. It was a wonder what people wanted.

No, the lady didn't Gift Aid. Sorry.

No bother.

"There're socks but no shoes" the woman said, as if she wanted to explain why. Norma nodded.

"The socks are mostly okay. No smelly feet!"

Norma smiled.

"Dad only had one foot" the young woman said, as Norma knew she would. People always did.

"So lots of them've hardly been worn."

"That's grand. Thank you, pet."

The birdlike old lady who had held the door open for her looked vaguely familiar, Betsy thought, now that she could see her properly. Obviously local from the way she spoke. Was she one of Dad's neighbours? She wasn't someone Betsy remembered from childhood but then she hadn't lived up here for so long. The women smiled at each other. Maz appeared from the back room as Betsy was letting herself out of the shop. She heard the exclamation of pleasure at the size of the donation, the hefty outlet of breath as the bags were lift-dragged off the shop floor into the sorting room and then, Ted had disappeared.

Now that the interminable requiem mass was over and Ted rested elsewhere, they were in the pub. Lizzie had organised it all; the landlord had agreed to supply sandwiches and nibbles on the understanding that Ted's lasses would be picking up the tab for the free-flowing alcohol that Ted's friends would down in his honour. Was it really just New Year's Eve when she had last been in there Betsy thought, standing aside from the group of celebrants determined to do justice to their dead mate? The same hideous patterned carpet, mismatched curtains, mdf oak-stained furniture that had collapsed so readily beneath the large man who had had the heart attack and they were all so busy with being happy that, at first, no one had noticed. She sipped her white wine – cold this time. The landlord had remembered her and planned accordingly; an astute commercial touch that had surprised Betsy. Lizzie said she was a snob and had been in Birmingham too long and that she had expected to see Betsy's fella at the funeral. What was his name? Something Irish or Scottish – definitely Celtic - Dad had said.

"Fergus".

"That's the one. So where is he?" Lizzie grinned.

"Working. Couldn't get away. He's an anaesthetist like me."

Lizzie continued to grin. She looked quite cheerful. "Even so" she said.

"It's not that kind of relationship" Betsy retorted, with as little expression as she could manage. And heard herself say it from the other side of the room.

Fergus could not wait for Betsy to get back. He had rung repeatedly to find out when she intended to return: it was essential that they went see Hugh Goldberg as soon as possible because thanks to JA, Phoebe's position was becoming untenable. As the anaesthetist in the now infamous bleeding IVC incident in theatre 4 in which JA had accused Phoebe of unwarranted interference, Betsy was urgently required to provide an account of what she had witnessed. She had had a ringside seat, had been there from start to finish and was a senior medic. Her word, if not law, would certainly carry weight – much more than those of the regs and surgical team. In his capacity in charge of clinical governance and chair of the most recent M&M meeting – from which Betsy had by necessity been absent – it had been, somehow, established (it was hard to define quite how) that Professor Dennington was a medical menace. No one said it; it was not written or documented but it was there, in every theatre, corridor and consulting room. In the canteen, staff rooms, even the darkest corners of the Imaging department (most of which Fergus was now familiar with). Even Phoebe felt it. The Ice Queen was in danger of melting.

Heather Eriksson was not a woman given to doubts; life was too busy, too short, too pressing, but even she was beginning to have concerns about Siobhan. They hardly ever saw her. Well, obviously not Graham who now spent most of his days upstairs and hardly saw anyone, but she and Archie, while perfectly happy with each other's company, were increasingly disconcerted by the girl's frequent absences. Where did she go? What did she do? It was not as if she was breaking any rules – she attended school (Heather had checked), came home on time at evenings and at weekends (especially weekends), ate reasonably well at proper meals with her mother and brother and did her share of household chores (without complaining). She was the model daughter but therein lay the problem. It seemed so .... unnatural. If only she would speak, communicate, even whinge or better still, take issue with something. But she said nothing beyond polite enquiries - the responses to which she did not listen – and basic civility. May I have the salt please or pass the butter did not count as conversation and even these had been curtailed to the point of giving up sugar in tea rather than having to ask for it across the table. Archie of course, dear boy, did not mind and more than compensated for his sibling's silence with all the chatter that he found most fascinating, fortunately to which neither Heather or Siobhan needed to listen. Only Siobhan's appearance suggested that there was a problem but no one, not even Heather, dared say anything. Her hair was darker, her complexion whiter, lips purpler, mascara heavier and expression more axe murderer. Often, she was accompanied by the scent of TCP which followed her like a familiar, catlike, rubbing itself against her black clad body. Heather suspected the presence of tattoos and piercings but could not prove it, not without some sort of physical assault, so the subject was left unmolested.

"Until Graham's better" Heather said to herself, already planning how she would approach the little madam. "When he gets his new liver, everything will get back to normal" she comforted herself. "It'll be just the way it was and we can all get on with our lives."

As soon as meals ended Siobhan excused herself and disappeared. Heather would have liked to follow her but sent Archie instead who merely reported that she had gone to her room via the bathroom or just to the bathroom. Sometime she went to see her father where she would sit on his bed – he had his own room these days. It had been Graham's idea – he was so restless in bed, he disturbed Heather who had such busy days and who needed her sleep. She did not argue but had carefully explained the reason for the - temporary - demise of the marriage bed to her offspring so as to offset any possibility of trauma or emotional turmoil. Archie had immediately seen the sense of the arrangement but Siobhan hadn't said a word, just stamped her Doc Martens up the stairs where they heard the bathroom door slam and the lock turn.

This morning - the same morning that in North Shields Betsy was depositing what was left of Ted in the charity shop, Heather had seen her daughter off to school as usual but had the unexpected pleasure of Archie being at home for once. Or twice. Archie felt the cold and was susceptible to infection. Although it was, thus far, undocumented, Heather was convinced that this was part of his condition. Heightened sensibilities, aversion to noise and change, acutely sensitive to texture and touch – it made sense that he would be more vulnerable physically than others so it was her duty to protect and nurture him. She understood that he did not want to wear heavy uncomfortable clothes so better to keep him in the warm than let him go out into the chill. Siobhan of course, seemed immune and wore virtually nothing to keep out the winter. Today Birmingham was at its most miserable. Grey, pinched and mean. Night and day seemed to have fused into one and although it was nearly lunch time, all the lights were on in the Eriksson's kitchen as Heather prepared something light and digestible for Graham, something without bits in for Archie and whatever was left from them both for herself.

"Take this up to Dad please, Archie" she said as she handed him the tray. "Don't worry" she comforted as he recoiled from it, "the tray's not hot to touch. You'll be fine. Take it steady" she encouraged as he picked his way across the floor towards the stairs. "You can do it."

Such a careful, such a thoughtful boy she congratulated herself as she listened to his feet slowly ascending step by step, then turned her attention to the contents of the fridge.

Even with her head in the fridge she was shocked by the noise. First the howl, then a gap, then Archie, shouting from the top of the stairs and all the way down as he flung himself onto each step with his full weight, not measuring the distance between his footsteps or counting the stairs as he went.

"There's blood, Mum. Dad's been sick and there's blood everywhere." He was still holding the tray. "I've spilled it" he howled anew.

CHAPTER TWENTY-THREE

Phoebe had been alerted of Graham Eriksson's imminent arrival as an emergency and asked to be paged as soon as the ambulance arrived. He was delivered by two paramedics as a swollen bloody parcel on a trolley at speed through the double doors and immediately incubated in the acute treatment area.

"Graham Eriksson. Blood filled vomit. Conscious but light headed. Primary biliary cirrhosis" announced the paramedic on his right as the one on the left tried to steer. The registrar picked up the pace by meeting the trolley head on as if taking a rugby catch and braced himself to kick it into touch.

"Page Professor Dennington" he shouted as he took the catch and and all three brought Graham to an abrupt halt so that the waiting team could attach, connect, stick, measure, monitor and intubate.

"Hello Graham. Professor Dennington's expecting you!" the registrar breezed. He could have been arriving for lunch Graham thought before he turned his head and retched voluminously over and along one side of the trolley. Blood spattered over the registrar's feet and shoes, then all over the floor. Graham would have liked to apologise for the mess but the retching would not stop.

"No one with him?"

"Wife said she'd follow. Childcare to sort."

The registrar's jollity was indomitable.

"No worries eh, Graham? We'll look after you" he beamed as he stepped out of a lumpy puddle. "Ah. Here's Professor Dennington."

Phoebe had indeed arrived, haste post haste but entirely unruffled, chignon intact, seamless and smooth. Her pencil skirt appeared to have been newly sharpened.

"Good afternoon, Graham" she greeted the invalid. He wondered if she was about to offer him a G&T before he ate. "Is your wife not with you? ... Oh well. Let's see what's going on, shall we?"

She was smiling as she began to press his stomach, issuing instructions for his admission and an endoscopy. He relaxed and closed his eyes.

Betsy had time to think as she drove towards Birmingham. She could have stayed longer in North Shields but Ted's flat was needed for someone else. They liked to have as quick a turnaround as possible the warden had explained – less unsettling for the other residents. Lizzie had organised the removal of Ted's effects (Why were they called effects? Betsy wondered. It made the deceased sound as if they had only ever been an illusion, a reflection, a magical trick.) There had been little enough; the house clearance company (one man with his brother's van) had not been impressed but had taken what "'e might be able to shift, pet, but not much in it". The stained carpets, thin curtains and chipped paintwork were bequeathed to the new occupant. Ironically however, everyone wanted the wheelchair, from the warden who could 'put it to good use' to the charity shop in the high street to which Betsy had taken the clothes where they had a notice in the window requesting all donations but especially wheelchairs, zimmers and commodes. Even the house clearance man said 'e always 'ad a buyer for a decent 'un, 'specially if it were collapsible.' Ted's, it seemed, was of more value than him and would certainly last longer.

The half-sisters had parted relatively amicably, possible because they were unlikely ever to meet again. There was nothing either of them wanted from the flat except that Lizzie took a few photographs of her mother and one of her parents on their wedding day. As there were none of Betsy's mother, she decided to leave empty handed. As she drove away, she took only the smell of the flat with her, embroidered into her clothes which she resolved to wash or discard as soon as she reached home.

Home. Birmingham. The hospital. Fergus.

She was still thinking about Fergus as she turned off the M1 onto the never ending A42 until it turned into the M42 and followed the signs and the traffic all the way into the city centre.

Phoebe and her patient – "please, call me Graham" – were getting on remarkably well. Graham was unusually forthcoming, almost bordering on chatty. Phoebe never quite reached that stage which suited them both perfectly, but the delivery of her analysis of Graham's condition was less ice, more melt water.

"The results of the endoscopy show that you have oesophageal varices ... Graham. This happens when the blood flow to your liver is blocked and the veins in your oesophagus enlarge and rupture. We've banded your varices to stop the bleeding and I'm confident you'll make a reasonable recovery, for the moment. However..." she paused. He waited. Looked at her. She looked back.

"The underlying cause is more concerning and indicates that your liver has significantly worsened."

"Meaning?"

The melt water stopped flowing for a moment and threatened to return to ice.

"Wouldn't you prefer to wait until your wife is here to have that discussion?" Phoebe could not bring herself to name the woman, but the question had to be asked.

"No. She's with the children ... Archie. He's... They'll be upset. Please. Just tell me."

To hide her surprise and possible relief (not that she would never admit to it) Phoebe shot from the hip.

"You need an urgent liver transplant. We need to operate while you are still well enough for the surgery so the first donor liver we receive will go to you... Unfortunately you no longer have the luxury of choice. However – and I'm sorry your wife is not here for this - you are now definitely at the top of the list."

There would be a wait of course. No one knew when an organ could become available but they would look after Graham in the hospital – there was no question of him going home until such time, hopefully, after a successful transplant. Phoebe would be on-call to perform the surgery ... and Ms Eriksson could contact her if she had had any questions. Yes, at any time. Reluctantly she handed over her mobile number but, well, Graham would tell his wife everything she needed to know in the first instance, wouldn't he? One of the team would make a point of popping in when Mrs Eriksson was there and bring them up to speed. All she had to do was ask someone at the ward desk to call through when she arrived. Yes, yes, Phoebe fully understood how important it was for Mrs Eriksson to be included in every discussion at every stage.

"Poor man" she said to the registrar as they walked away.

A quick visit to her flat – gated, third floor, new build, balcony, three bedrooms (two ensuite) wooden floors, Scandi-style white light flow – while she changed, put on the washing machine and checked her post then Betsy was back in the car heading as quickly as traffic permitted towards the hospital; and Fergus. There was work to be done. He had kept in touch in a perfunctory sort of way and she knew that he had been covering her schedule assiduously. That was good news and no more than she had expected. Nevertheless, she felt outside things, externalised, irrelevant. It was time to get back and be indispensable before she was forgotten. That was how it worked – God knows she had seen it often enough. It wasn't that people weren't valued or wanted but the pace of the place, the pressure, the stress meant that if you were off the radar you disappeared. Out of sight. There was a multitude of ambitious registrars eyeing up consultancy (and private practice) like an army in waiting, pacing the land, looking to intercept and pounce. Maybe even Fergus would be tempted; he wasn't getting any younger. The stability might be appealing even to his peripatetic nature. It was never a boring job. As he would no doubt have discovered. She pressed down on the accelerator.

"Betsy!"

He seemed pleased to see her. Uncharacteristically demonstrative. It was rather touching and she relaxed into a smile. Nothing public though.

"Fergus."

"We've missed you."

Really? He looked as if he meant it. All scrubbed up and ready to go he said he was on his way to assist Phoebe Dennington – nothing special, routine, dull, bread and butter stuff – but he had to step out for a moment to see her. How could he not? Besides, now that she was back there was so much they had to do.

She looked. He continued.

The debacle over Phoebe was ongoing and getting worse. They had to do something, soon. He would make an appointment with Hugh Goldberg (he was rummaging in his pocket for his phone which should not have been there but, well, this was Fergus. At least it was on silent.) Betsy noticed that it was vibrating and shivering, as if it had goose bumps. He kept the caller hidden as he pressed the end call button and started to look for the Medical Director's number. Betsy hadn't yet got back into the schedule… she was available asap? He would ensure that he could fit in with any time suggested. They really had to act; Phoebe's position was becoming untenable and JA was out of control. He might have been describing a political coup. However, he had been doing some 'research' of his own into JA: past cases, statistics, that sort of thing. Phoebe would be fine – totally vindicated - if he and Betsy handled this the right way. It all hung on that IVC resection where Betsy had been present. Her testimony was crucial; he couldn't wait for her to get back. How was she? Did the funeral go alright?

She watched him as he made his way back towards theatre 4, talking to his phone, neat buttocked, solid thighs, muscularly developed calves evident even in the saggy blue polycotton of his trousers. Trust Fergus to wear a pair slightly too small unlike everyone else who opted for comfort and freedom of movement. She wondered, briefly, to whom he was talking and then found, to her relief, that it did not matter.

CHAPTER TWENTY-FOUR

When news of the availability of a donor liver less than three days later was conveyed to Graham, Heather was with him. So was Archie who preferred not to be left at home but there was no sign of Siobhan who preferred to be wherever her mother was not. Besides, she could ring her Dad any time and did. It was so much easier to talk to him when it was just the two of them.

Phoebe and Ann Williams had delivered the news together; safety in numbers although neither said as much. They stood, side by side, walled, ready. We shall not be moved. Phoebe would take the lead with Ann prepared to intervene and reinforce where necessary. They had as much information about the condition of the liver as was possible at this stage; feared the worst but found strength in the knowledge that this was Graham's last chance so resistance was futile. But would Heather know that?

"So all being well with your bloods and pre-op and the organ retrieval, I plan to operate later today." Phoebe spoke directly to Graham, carefully blinkering Heather out of view. Ann also focused exclusively on Graham although she wore the presence of wife and even son like an overtight pair of trousers, squeezing her waist, rearranging her knickers and itching her legs.

"You're very lucky that we have an organ so quickly. Very lucky indeed" Phoebe continued as Ann nodded in agreement. Graham clearly agreed which was encouraging as he too nodded his head with almost as much enthusiasm as the Recipient Co-ordinator. Then there was silence as they waited. It was only a matter of time.

It was Archie, not Heather, who spoke.

"I suppose the condition of the liver is immaterial at this stage."

It could have been a question but it was difficult to know; Archie always spoke like that. Somewhere between the judgement of Solomon and a level of humility required in public to meet standards of politeness and to avoid causing offence. Of course, he knew the answer – he always did – but one had to be seen to be making suitable conversation and adapting one's intellect to the company in which one found oneself – that's what his mother had taught him.

Phoebe and Ann grasped the proffered straw and clung on.

"Yes" Phoebe barked.

"I'm afraid so" Ann consoled.

"That's it then" said Graham.

Everyone looked at the bench.

"Yes" Heather ruled.

The room breathed, Ann's trousers were suddenly more comfortable, Archie nodded sagely with all the wisdom of Cassandra and the transplant was set to go ahead. Graham would call his daughter and tell her the news, hoping that she would brave her mother and come to see him before he went into theatre. He signed the consent forms there and then; Heather's signature was not required.

Fergus would have liked to be the anaesthetist for the transplant. He loved working with Phoebe. So calm, measured, ordered and organised. Personally, he preferred some sort of musical accompaniment in theatre, especially when it was long haul, but Phoebe was the lead surgeon and it was her call. Her gig as it were. He would have liked to see the rhythm of her movement echoed in sounds other than the suck slop glub of the procedure, punctuated only by pithy instruction-commands. Phoebe did not do chat over the table. Betsy however did not seem to mind and was looking forward to getting back to work. Proper work, where she could concentrate and forget Fergus and her father, where she could adjust her breathing to blend with that of the ventilator and fix her gaze on her inert green-sheeted subject, speaking to her through screens and monitors.

"At least we've got an appointment with Hugh Goldberg" Fergus consoled himself. He had arranged it with the redoubtable Debbie, with whom he had been careful to establish an unimpeachably chaste flirtatious rapport on the grounds that she seemed to have some sort of equally irreproachable hotline to the Medical Director. A bizarre arrangement in Fergus's eyes which amounted to a massively missed opportunity, but one which could be exploited nevertheless. He and Betsy were scheduled to meet Hugh the following morning, first thing. Debbie had been wonderfully accommodating. It meant that Betsy was likely to have a late night what with a transplant, the immediate follow up and catching up on what she had missed during her sojourn in the north. But that was the name of the game; she would understand and Hugh Goldberg was seeing them ahead of his existing schedule. Squeezed in, literally, by Debbie, Fergus was pleased. It was also useful that Betsy would be fresh from theatre where Phoebe had presided: her witness statement would be that much more pertinent. They were due to meet Hugh at 7.45. He would meet Betsy there.

She was late.

"Where the hell is she?" Fergus hissed at his watch which only shrugged and carried on ticking. Not his problem.

At 7.47 the door to Hugh's office opened and his head appeared around it, strangely detached, as if it had decided to take a walk without the rest of his body. Eyes peered over glasses under a shelf of red hair.

"Come in" the mouth said and the head disappeared.

"Dr Jones will be here in a minute" Fergus said as he followed.

"No problem. There's something I wanted to discuss with you first anyway" answered the voice from within.

The door closed behind him. It was still closed when Betsy finally arrived, fifteen minutes later. Should she knock? As she hesitated Debbie appeared and suggested that she take a seat. The Medical Director would not be long; there was something he had to discuss with Dr Crombie and he would let her know when Betsy was required.

Required? Betsy thought. Ouch. She pulled out her phone to examine her texts and sat down to wait.

Ten minutes later Debbie looked up from her computer screen and announced that Betsy could go into the office. She checked that her phone was on silent and duly obeyed the summons, 'required' at last. Inside the office she found Fergus seated gladiatorially opposite Hugh Goldberg who stood up to greet her. Fergus stayed put; did not even look at her.

"Betsy. How are you? I'm so sorry to hear about your recent bereavement. Please, take a seat." The Medical Director was all solace and affability. "I hope this won't take long. I just want to hear your account of the er, events, in theatre 4 concerning Mr Albright and Professor Dennington."

That was easy and did not indeed, take long. Betsy was more than happy to provide a written account to support her narrative; no, she had never had anything but praise for Professor Dennington and although they were not 'friends' and did not mix socially outside the hospital, she had never had any cause to complain about the professor at any level. Yes, she was always happy to work with her in theatre and ... if she might proffer an opinion, so was everyone else. 'Except JA' hung unspoken, elephantine, in the air, looking from one to another, waving its trunk as if to deny the charge.

Fergus took up the challenge.

"He's orchestrating a campaign to deliberately undermine her. He's trying to discredit her without cause or foundation, abusing his position as Lead for Clinical Governance to rake up past incidents, all of which have been documented and shelved. Ancient history – and none of it was relevant in the first place... He's out to get her."

Betsy gaped. Fergus ignored her. Hugh's eyebrows lost contact with his glasses which were trying to escape off the end of his nose – anything to avoid the embarrassment of the moment.

"That is a very serious allegation, Dr Crombie. Can it be substantiated?"

It could and it was.

Fergus went on to identify two separate occasions when one death and another near miss had been experienced as a direct result of JA's incompetence and lack of leadership. His arrogance. Procrastination. Propensity to panic. Abuse of position in that he had deliberately concealed the reality of the situations in his capacity of overseeing clinical governance. Everyone – especially Phoebe Dennington – except JA himself was subjected to the most stringent investigation and documentation. He even seemed to keep files on everyone for 'future' use.

And yes, he interjected as Hugh tried to plead moderation, there was plenty of evidence to support his allegations. Names, dates, places, medical details would all be provided. All the Medical Director had to do was follow them up and ask the right questions. With that he got to his feet, looked straight past Betsy, turned his back on the desk, the MD, his future at the hospital and left the room.

He went straight to find Phoebe. She was in her cubby hole, emailing *The American Journal of Transplantation*. One of her registrars had been working on a new idea in warm machine perfusion of the retrieved liver. His research was extensive and thorough in support of a concept (patent applied for) that was topical, innovative and very marketable. Hugely marketable. Hence her approach to the American publication – its British counterpart could pick it up later when it was in the commercial domain. The registrar would become both rich and a consultant on the back of it for which Phoebe was glad although she was even more pleased that she could put her name to it – alongside that of the registrar, naturally – and would also make a great deal of money as well as achieving the kind of recognition that her colleagues could only dream of. Especially Jeremy Albright. And Hugh Goldberg. An idea, after all, was just that unless one had the wherewithal to promote, develop and nurture the concept to fruition. Her reg was sensible enough to recognise how much she owed her mentor and they had agreed at the outset that this was very much a joint venture. Now Phoebe could make her contribution and deliver the baby to the world.

Fergus was an unwelcome interruption. Didn't he have work to do? Somewhere to be? In a helicopter or something? She did not even look up from the screen when he pushed open the door – hadn't even tapped on it by way seeking admission she noticed and swallowed her lips.

"Phoebe."

"Fergus".

"Can we speak?"

"Now?"

"Yes... Please."

She was the one tapping now, vigorously on the keyboard, trying to finish her train of thought. It was important to phrase things succinctly but with flair and panache for the American Journal. They were notoriously difficult to persuade and this was an opportunity she could not afford to lose. Still, Fergus had said please which was unusual. She sighed and got to then end of her sentence. As she stabbed the full stop she lifted her head and angled it in his direction. He could not quite see her face but this could not wait.

"I've just seen Hugh Goldberg."

"Oh, yes?" This was more interesting than usual for Fergus. "About what?"

A short silence. Phoebe started to re-read her email.

"I've been given a formal warning."

Now she looked at him, properly, turning her whole body so that she could get him into full view.

"What for?"

Not 'that's ridiculous' or 'outrageous' or 'has he lost his mind' or anything that might reflect the absurd injustice of the situation and Fergus' undoubted innocence, but an enquiry as to why, Fergus noticed. He felt cold and wanted to sit down, but there really wasn't all that much room. So he perched on the side of her desk and they looked at each other.

"Sexual harassment."

"Who?"

The cold became more intense, tightening his stomach. Not a

word of indignation or dissent from you, he thought. What the hell was the matter with the woman?

"Some FY1. I don't even know her fucking name."

Phoebe winced – she loathed effing and blinding, as well he knew.

"Well did you?"

"No! It's a complete misinterpretation. The silly bitch is paranoid. It was just harmless banter once or twice, nothing more. But she's over reacted and complained and it's gone all the way up the line to the fu... "he stopped himself, "to our illustrious Medical Director, who has to be seen to do something, so he's given me a warning."

"Verbal?"

"Yes. Bastard."

"Your first?"

"Yes! No one's ever complained before, not to my knowledge. I don't understand it."

Phoebe did. Fergus had a reputation. The only real surprise was that it had taken this long to be formally recognised.

"What will you do?" she asked.

Could she not see that whatever he decided to do depended on her?

"Will you leave?" Phoebe turned back to her screen and her email while Fergus stared at the side of her face, which suddenly seemed sharp. Angular. Less sculpted and more pointed. Thin. Mean. The perfect chignon, the discreet earrings so easy to remove or tape over when operating, the high cheekbones that he so admired.

"You may have no choice, not if you want to get on."

"Fuck you Phoebe".

Now she did look up, but he was no longer there.

CHAPTER TWENTY-FIVE

"Please, Siobhan. For me."

Graham was begging from his bed. Sitting up, not yet able to go on bended knee but not far off. His new liver was – he touched the wooden frame of the bedside locker – doing well. Holding. Working. Settling in.

"It's a new start for us all. She only did what she thought best."

Siobhan looked at her pink-faced father, a tube up his nose, coloured coded tubes jutting out of his neck, tied by yet another tube to a bag of saline dripping into his narrow arm. He looked like a roughly torn stick of celery, all ridges and tatty ends. His eyes were enormous.

"You could've died, Dad."

"But I didn't and now I'm not going to. ... They'll be here in a minute."

Less. Heather and Archie were already appearing at the entrance of the HDU, mother slightly ahead of son, leading the way until she saw her daughter when she faltered but did not stop. Archie bowled past her to find a chair for himself which he placed at the end of the bed where he could examine the mechanics that made it constantly vibrate to prevent bed sores. So clever. The movement was barely discernible but seemed to work, although there had been a less savoury moment when Graham, high on morphine had misinterpreted the sensation and thought the ceiling was falling in on him while the supporting walls were making run for it. He was still hallucinating but becoming more accustomed to it now. Anything to alleviate the pain. but fear came in many forms. He watched his wife.

Heather marched over to his bedside and stood there, sentinel. How was he? He looked alright. Pain still bad? Something would have to be done she determined as he filed his report and she looked for something to sit on. It was while she was running her finger along the top of the bag of saline checking for dust when noise on the other side of the bed caught her attention. Siobhan was standing up and moving aside so that her mother could sit down, close to the patient. Without a word Siobhan went to find another chair while Heather placed herself close beside her husband so that she could tidy him up and keep an eye on the nursing staff. Graham inhaled deeply and did not even wince at the extra pain caused. Pain was a way of life. Heather said it was intolerable and had to be dealt with but for him it was a friend - it reminded him that he was alive.

It was Heather who spotted Phoebe in the doorway first and could fix her gaze on the surgeon as she too marched over to Graham's bed. There was another woman with her whom Heather did not recognize. Younger, blonder, less expensive, obviously more junior but smart nevertheless – a consultant? Or merely a wannabe?

"Mrs Eriksson. How nice. How are you? May I introduce Dr Jones who was the consultant anaesthetist at your husband's transplant. She has a special interest in post-operative pain in liver transplant patients and is keen to talk to Graham about his experience."

"He's in agony. It's intolerable. We weren't prepared for this. We were told to expect some pain, yes, but not this. My husband's suffering dreadfully and I want to know what you intend to do about it. ... There's no sign of any nursing staff. Where are they all?"

It was tempting to say that they had seen Heather when she arrived on the ward and, to a body, had been urgently required elsewhere. So busy, short staffed, patient care, paperwork, they couldn't possibly be everywhere at once; it was a particularly busy time; someone was always available though so Graham need not worry.

"So what are you going to do to stop the pain?" Heather had turned her attention to Betsy who was ready. Forewarned by Phoebe she was well armed.

"We're going to set him up with a morphine PCA – patient controlled analgesia – which is a machine with a button to press that releases morphine doses programmed by the anaesthetist. Which is why I'm here" Betsy said directly to Graham. "I want to find out what you need." She smiled encouragingly. Heather glared.

"You're a consultant?"

"I am." Betsy turned the smile on Heather but it was stony ground. Fortunately Siobhan had arrived back, chairless, like a dusky angel. Batlike she spread out her arms and spoke to her mother.

"Let's go and get a coffee" she suggested. "C'mon Archie", knowing that her mother would be bound to follow where her brother went, that he did not drink coffee and would insist on something else which would have to be vetted and approved by his adoring maternal parent. Everyone except Heather began to smile. Archie beamed at the prospect of a hot chocolate and started to plot how he could wangle an extra-cream-with-marshmallow topping.

As the two consultants left Graham, relaxing into his pillows, they started to discuss Phoebe's warm perfusion project. It was about to enter the phase two safety and tolerability trials in patients for the first time Phoebe said, and that was where Betsy came in,

"To provide anaesthetic support and input." Would she be interested?

She would. Since returning to work Betsy had seen little of Fergus and wanted to see him less. Phoebe had not seen him at all but had heard that his application for a full-time position with the air ambulance service had been accepted with immediate effect. Hugh Goldberg had told her himself when she had been summoned to his office to discuss the situation with JA. This had been a surprise. What situation? Of course, she had been aware of a certain coldness among her colleagues towards her but no, it had not caused any adverse effect and it most definitely had not interfered with her work. Nothing ever did. She was far too professional for such a thing. If JA had had an issue with her, why on earth had he not spoken to her about it? Hugh refrained from comment at this point. If anything, it was Phoebe who ought to have issues with JA she said and Hugh found it difficult not to nod in agreement. Instead he focussed on her chignon over his glasses, waited for her to finish speaking then informed her that she had always had his full confidence and that he was interested in her latest research. Which registrar was doing it?

It was one of those weirdly beautiful winter days when the sun was warm and it felt as if Spring had arrived early, testing the water, in half a mind to unpack and settle in. Norma was not in the shop today – she did four days a week which left her two days for the house and shopping then one for visiting Alan.

Sometimes she didn't bother much with shopping – how much could a small bird eat? – but she always kept the house just the clean, organised way Alan had liked it. Everything in its place, pet. Since she had started spending Saturdays in the shop the weekends no longer weighted her down and clipped her wings. She could fly if she chose, not that she would have gone far. Not without Alan. But Sunday was still their day, just as it always had been. Not so much the paper in front of the fire while a joint roasted in the oven (enough for two with cold cuts on Monday, just like her Mam taught her) but a milky coffee mid-morning before she put on her best coat and headed off to the cemetery with the carrier bag that lived, ready, packed and waiting, on the same hook as her coat. No cut flowers – Alan always said they were a waste – but usually she took a small trowel in the carrier bag with the thermos and a bite to eat, as well as her best handbag. (The one Alan had bought – real leather with an enamel clasp) She liked to tidge and tidy his grave while they chatted. However, this Sunday she left the trowel on the hall stand, below Alan's coat, scarf and hat and barely noticed it as she stepped out onto the pavement and shut the door behind her.

"It's from the lady who's got your liver, pet. She's called..." Norma scanned the letter she was holding and adjusted her reading glasses all the better to see. "Amber. Amber Kowalski. Such a pretty name." She stopped to give Alan time to absorb the information. He liked to take his time, mull things over before saying anything. Thoughtful. Then when he spoke it was worth the saying and the hearing.

"She's got a partner ... Agwe ... not a name I know but no bother, and they have two bairns. Two bairns Alan! Think of it! Let me read you what she says..." she adjusted her bottom on the tartan rug she had spread on the ground and stretched out her legs. A picnic for two but only one.

'How can we ever thank you? I am alive and healthy, thanks to you. My children have a mother as well as a father. We have a future as a family together and we owe it all to you and your husband.'

"That's you, Alan. It's your liver she's got. ... and..." here she gripped the letter so hard it crumpled in protest "she wants to meet us! With the bairns, who're only little. Because, she says ... 'now we are part of their family too.' Oh Alan. Bairns. Just like we always wanted."

Printed in Great Britain
by Amazon

48526960R00136